CLIMBIÉ

BERNARD B. DADIÉ

translated by
Karen C. Chapman

C1

AFRICANA PUBLISHING CORPORATION
NEW YORK

Published in the United States of America 1971
by Africana Publishing Corporation
101 Fifth Avenue
New York, N.Y. 10003

Library of Congress Catalog Card No. 77–161231

ISBN 0–8419–0089–2 (paper)
0080–9 (cloth)

Set in Linotype Granjon and
Printed in Great Britain by
Cox & Wyman Ltd, London, Fakenham and Reading

TRANSLATOR'S NOTE

TO RENDER such complex poetic vision in English is the challenge Dadié's translator must face. Particulars likely to be obscure, of African history and society, are explained in the footnotes. For help with these, and for so much else, I would like to thank Mr Dadié and Mr Ezekiel Mphahlele. I should, above all, like to thank my husband Jerry, who guided me.

IN THE N'Zima dialect *climbié* means 'some other day', *un jour plus tard*.

FOREWORD

IT HAS BECOME a habit for us these days to complain that intellectuals – including writers, artists, politicians, and scholars – from French-speaking Africa do not work smoothly with those from countries of British influence in Africa. Somehow when we are in conferences, we find ourselves talking along parallel lines, or we find argument entangled in fluent, passionate rhetoric, or else served up in a highly prosaic manner, lacking any kind of romance. In small groups we say of one another, 'Oh those francophones, they're the end!' and 'Les anglophones – c'est véritablement la mentalité anglo-saxonne, ça!' Yet we keep coming to a meeting point somewhere: the times demand it, the ideals of pan-Africanism, however depressingly distant they often look, make it desperately necessary for us to understand one another, if only at the basic colour level.

Among the various avenues we seek towards practical cooperation and solidarity, like introducing African-French literature to English-speaking communities and African-English literature in francophone Africa, a translation like Mrs Chapman's of *Climbié* is a most significant milestone. There has been a tendency, once an African-French novel has been translated into English, for the translator to stay with the particular author and work on his other novels. This is only natural. Thus a few titles have been translated of Cameroun's Mongo Beti and Ferdinand Oyono, Guinea's Camara Laye. We expect to see more translations of Sembène Ousmane than the one that exists. And we already have a sizeable number of African poets of French expression in English. We hope French-speaking scholars and writers will make available to their communities much more

African-English writing – at least as much as they have done Afro-American literature.

Although we in Africa write in diverse traditions – French, English, Portuguese, etc. – what we write is culturally accessible outside a particular tradition on the continent. Village and city experiences in Africa have much in common. Then there is the common colonial and post-colonial experience, the common exposure to industrialization and technology, the common politics of nation-building and so on. A progressively greater measure of exposure to one another's literatures in translation must in the long run advance the pan-African cause. For this, again, Mrs Chapman deserves our thanks. Already she is planning a translation of Dadié's *Le Pagne Noir*.

Francophone Africa has done much more to record folklore than the English-speaking side. Bernard Dadié passionately believes that African stories, legends, proverbs should be retold in their original languages and recorded. They are 'a lesson in prudence, generosity, patience and wisdom, indispensable to the guidance of mankind and the stability of society'. He also believes that they can influence African writing today, in themes and styles. *Le Pagne Noir* and *Légendes Africaines*, which are volumes of traditional tales, are one such effort to arrest the fast disappearance of the art of oral narrative and the moral values intrinsic to traditional lore. In this drive Dadié is supported by men like Ahmadu Hampaté Ba, the Islamic scholar of Mali, and Birago Diop, the Senegalese poet, the Dahomean writers Jahen Alapini and Alexandre Adandé.

Like so many other French-speaking Africans, Dadié is continuously asserting the beauty of African life as a constant reminder that colonialism cheated the black man out of his heritage. He says in one of his poems, 'I will weave a crown for you with a gentle glow, with the lustre of Venus of the tropics. And I will write your name in flaming letters, O Africa, in the sphere of the milky way's agitated twinkle.' He writes elsewhere again, 'I thank you, God, for having made me black, for having made me the sum of all the sorrows.'

And yet this assertion is not a posturing with Dadié, or an

attempt to make rhetoric do the feeling for him. His is a tough confrontation with alienation and the need to strike a delicate balance between the frivolous and the genuine impulses *d'aller en pèlerinage aux sources*. Dadié, like Senghor, is more cosmopolitan than many people would imagine when they observe the fierceness of some of these men's poetic yearnings. The 'romantic agony' for the African lies along the way he must pick through the vast landscape of anti-colonial ideologies, technological imperatives, poverty, ignorance, disease – the way that must share in both our living traditions and alien values that we have appropriated as our own. I insist that without this agony, our literary expression is mere slick, comfortable, convenient posturing.

Climbié, like the other prose works of its family, portrays the quality of African childhood experiences. The general outlines of the pattern are common: tough elementary education, dogged by poverty, sadistic schoolmastership, and so on; life among the many relatives in the African extended family; childhood ambitions; secondary education which is perpetually haunted by the fear of failure; the day one sets out in pursuit of one's vision; new experiences in the encounter with white authority that invariably suspects and fears the 'educated native'.

Nothing spectacular happens to Climbié until he has finished secondary school and is working – towards the end of the book.

His development is like the muted process of plant growth in which the seed germinates, pushes through, always in an upward thrust, until it blossoms and lays bare its foliage, now exposed to wind, sun, rain, insects that lie in wait for its juices, in a way it never happened before. As with the plant, things happen to Climbié; he never 'happens' to them, until he reacts to white domination once he is back home from Senegal. His development is fully rendered by the marvellously subtle shift in Dadié's style, especially in Part II; the style 'grows up' with Climbié. And yet, again, like a plant, he is part of the landscape which we view through him. Dadié has portrayed for us, often in a volatile idiom that reflects his mercurial personality, a human and physical landscape that is alive, at once friendly and hostile, and indifferent.

Often, even the matter-of-fact descriptions Dadié gives cut like a rapier, whether they are regarded as humorous or not:

> On Sunday mornings the church was filled with the faithful, but one would see very few Whites there.
> The Europeans, tired of reciting 'Our Father Who Art In Heaven, Give Us Our Daily Bread', had without a doubt either decided to get this bread without the help of the 'Father', or, simply satiated, preferred to sleep all morning. . . .

Again:

> Ah, these Whites! Do you remember the story about the cashier, the one about the lumberman, and . . . Will we never stop telling stories about disillusioned Whites who kill themselves in Africa? Because a fiancée hasn't answered a letter, bang! someone kills himself. Because money is missing from the cashbox, bang! someone kills himself. . . .

Having said what a valuable contribution Mrs Chapman's sensitive and sympathetic translation is to the pan-African ideal, I must not forget to stress its importance to American scholarship and imagination of Africa. Interest in African studies, including the languages and literatures of the continent, is increasing among both English and American readers. I know that Bernard Dadié's moving *récit* will add another dimension to their understanding of Africa, and perhaps of themselves.

Ezekiel Mphahlele
University of Zambia
Lusaka, Zambia

PART I

CLIMBIÉ dropped the stub of charcoal he was using for chalk, parted two pickets in the fence, jumped over piles of rubbish, and struck out. He ran straight before him. In his ears echoed the imperious voice of the schoolmaster, who had just shouted at two roguish boys: 'Bring that sandfly back here!' His forefinger was raised aggressively at the end of his arm, like the bayonet on a musket ready to belch its leaden charge.

Climbié did not wait for the rest of the sentence before taking to the open. He had barely glimpsed the schoolmaster's head at the window when his heart bounded. Already Climbié had heard him say: 'Make off, make off fast, before I brain you!'

The sand screaked under the feet of the two 'big' boys sent after him. Climbié could hear their panting, and imagined that he felt their fingers grab him by the neck. Teeth clenched, fists knotted into balls, eyes wide open and fixed straight ahead, he ran. He must not be the first to tire. He wanted to turn around sharply, and with a fistful of sand blind those two following him. Oh, if only he had miraculous powers, like those strange beings talked about in legends! He would disappear then, right in front of their eyes.

The wind howled in his ears and tried to brake his pace; his heart pounded against his rib-cage, unable to smash through and clear a passage for itself.

That schoolmaster, only yesterday he had thrashed a student until he bled. Climbié had seen him, and the memory gave him wings. Oh no, he wasn't going to be beaten bloody, not him! He rushed on, regardless of where he put his feet, for his feet had acquired eyes. His body? He could not feel it. Everything in him took part in this escape: buttocks, back, trunk, legs, arms, head; everything in him fled from the blows of the schoolmaster's rattan walking-stick.

Climbié was sick and tired of a school which forbade children to write on the walls, which were like big slates. Laboriously each child would draw one letter, two letters, which, keeping his head down, he would then admire, satisfied with the progress he had made. Then he would erase and start over again, to train his hand. To get a score of eighteen in handwriting was not easy, and it was even harder to get one of those high marks which any student likes to show off. So one erased. It would dirty the wall a little, that's all. Is it so bad to write on the walls of a school? A child's joy in learning, the enthusiasm that sweeps him up, directs his hands. The keen appetite to learn, the passionate desire to read through the textbooks rapidly, all of them, compels him to take the charcoal between his fingers, makes him stick out his tongue and lower his head. All that, alas, is not understood by grown-ups. If you cannot write on the walls of a school, then what walls can you write on? Really now, grown-ups, usually so thoughtful, are no longer so when they have to deal with youngsters. . . .

Climbié had at first written on the sand the mysterious letters of the alphabet. It was easy to get them confused, although each had its own name. Then the wind had come and erased them. If the wind had remained calm, nothing would have happened, and Climbié would not have at his heels those two scamps determined to take him back to the schoolmaster.

What was more, the wall was not messed up; the letters were properly written. . . . What harm had he done? Why were they running after him? Well then, there wouldn't be any harm to *him*. He wouldn't get a beating.

Climbié kept running. On one side, the ocean raised its voice to frighten him since he wanted to throw himself in; on the other side, were small huts and alleys.

Would he have enough strength to reach the village? Those bloodhounds following him were gaining ground with each step.

He ran, determined to escape, to run to the mouth of the Comoé river, to the end of the world, to his last breath, until the other

[2]

two ceased to follow him or until he dropped dead from exhaustion. . . . It was settled: he would not reappear alive before that schoolmaster.

Disturbed by Climbié's approach, some feasting pigs grunted but beat a retreat. Broken bottles, pieces of scrap iron, nails – nothing hurt him; even the convolvulus didn't trip him up. Everything seemed to favour his flight. . . . Should he return? No! He must flee. . . . The walking-stick! The blood! Yes, he must escape. But his feet could no longer drag along his body, now heavy with fatigue. . . . Thank God for the old man approaching! He was smoking a pipe; in his hand was the bulb of an enema syringe. Climbié headed straight for him, grabbed him with both arms, and asked for protection. The boys chasing him also stopped; they talked with the old man for a long time; then they retraced their steps, making clear to Climbié, with gestures of the head and fingers, that they would wait for him at school the next day. Climbié let them go. Taking a thousand detours, startled by every encounter, checking each alley-way before entering it, he returned home.

Climbié never went back to that school where children were cruelly beaten, where every evening after class they had to go to the seashore and empty the latrine buckets.

AT THE CAMP Climbié helped his uncle N'dabian with each task. By his uncle's side, he was learning a man's work. When the fires were lit, to prepare the soil Climbié would throw twigs on the blaze, for he loved watching the smoke rise and drown the forest, and listening to the eagle sing high above at noon, when everything was aglow. Climbié went from one fire to another, sweating in the heat. His uncle N'dabian kept shouting: 'Watch out! Don't burn yourself!' He climbed on the bushes, slid, fell, and scratched himself. Crying, he limped away and sat down in the shade of a large tree. There, armed with a stick, he tormented the insects, ants, worms, and centipedes. Dragon-flies, green and yellow, buzzed above the rust-coloured ponds. A lizard drew near boldly and frightened him, then ran to save itself. A bird flew up, then settled elsewhere. Huge dragon-flies with long red and ashy-blue spindles pursued him incessantly. Butterflies looted the flowers. Under the large tree, the workers huddled together, and after eating and drinking, they chatted or napped before starting to work again.

When the first rains came, it was time to sow the rice, plant bananas, pimentos, eggplants, sugar-cane, and fruit trees. During the heaviest part of the rainy season, the coffee and cocoa were transplanted.

Coffee trees were afraid of weeds, while cocoa plants feared both the weeds and the sun. Dying cocoa trees with burned leaves were found every day. These had to be replaced. At weeding-time the workers, either through carelessness or spite, cut some of the healthy coffee and cocoa plants; these also had to be replaced. There was a veritable race between the planted trees and the rank weeds which, full of sap, drew their vitality from the sun, and sprang up again within a week after they had been cut. They clambered over the tops of the cultivated plants and covered them, suffocating them and stopping them from growing.

Sometimes the rains came late. And this was a disaster. But if the rains came too soon, this was still a disaster, for they would knock the flowers off the coffee plants, thus lessening production. And always, Uncle N'dabian had his eyes fixed on the weather, on the sun, the moon, and the stars. He knew, within two or three days, just by watching the sky, when the rains would come, when the sea turtle would crawl to the beach and lay its eggs, when such and such a fish would be plentiful. When the stars shone red, he predicted the coming of terrible events.

And Climbié, who loved to stretch out in his uncle's lap, also looked up at the sky, and followed the finger that pointed out for him the myriad stars, the stars that blinked as if they were tired of shining, the stars that brought drought or else a profusion of snails. . . .

'Do you see the moon's heir? That's the star that always attends her. It knows all her stories. It never leaves her, whereas among people in this country, an heir never comes to help you with your work. He waits until you drop before he comes to take his place. My nephew, my heir, is a maker of palm-wine. He doesn't yet know how to plant, and even less how to take care of coffee and cocoa. If I died tomorrow, what would he do?'

'You will never die, Papa.'

'Why?'

'Because you are good.'

'Do you think Death is aware of that? She just comes and takes you.'

'I'll fight her.'

'You won't see her.'

'Yes I will, and I'll give her a pounding on the face, mouth, and chest, and she'll run to save herself, over there, on the other side of the river.'

'And if, in spite of all your violence, she got me anyhow, what would you do?'

'Me! I'd die with you. . . . We would leave together, and every night I would go to sleep on your lap, and you would tell me marvellous stories. Where do the stars come from?'

'God made them.'

'With what? And where is God anyway?'

'A long, long time ago, God lived among men, and they could see him just as you see me. But one day, an old woman who was grinding salt struck the heavens with her pestle. Then God got mad and went away . . . far away . . . over there. . . .'

'Where over there?'

'Up there, way, way up high, and from that day on, men were no longer happy, because God was no longer with them.'

'Oh! Why did the old woman do that?'

'In those days too, all creatures lived together. There was a kind of bird, now extinct, whose wings made a shade over the whole village. One day, finding the world full of injustices, he left the village and went to live somewhere else. He lived there alone for many years. Then, one morning, three strangers came to him.

'The first had barely finished saying: "I am the son of God," when the bird got violently angry. "Get out of here, you son of

[5]

injustice! I know no one in the world more unjust than your father. Look! He made some creatures with two feet, others with four, and still others who have to crawl because they have no legs. Is that just? Why didn't he give every creature either two feet or four? Some creatures are beautiful, and others are repulsively ugly! Why? Some are rich; others are poor! Some are red, blue, or white; others are black or violet. Will I ever finish listing all the injustices of your father? Why is there this preference among creatures?"

'The second stranger came forward: "I am the son of Plague."

'The bird's anger no longer knew any bounds.

' "Make off! Go away! Get out of my house, you son of a vulture . . .! Your father is even more unjust than God. He takes one person's eye and another person's ear. . . . He is dead set on bringing misfortune to some, while others are bursting with health, for all to see. He makes some deaf, some blind, and tortures them from birth, while he lets others enjoy life in peace. . . . Get out of here at once, before I break your back!"

'Finally, the third stranger presented himself: "I am the son of Death."

' "Come, my friend . . ." said the bird, opening his wings and enfolding him. "Let me embrace you. Your father is the only just man I know. Whether God made you beautiful or ugly, he takes you: whether you are rich or poor, weak or strong, blue, white, black, or red, he takes you. He respects no one. Before him alone are all men equal." '

'But Death, isn't he also unjust?'

'And way up there, they debated which one of the fathers was the most just or the most unjust.'

Climbié gazed up at the stars, these old stars for ever young, the moon for ever beautiful, with its shadowy drummer-boy. He studied them and tried to count them, but each time he had to start over again, because some timid stars never shone the way they were supposed to, and he always made a mistake.

'Don't count them, my son,' Papa N'dabian said, while running his hands through his hair. 'That's not good.'

'Why?'

'You would have to count them all, or else die, because the other stars would be unhappy.'

They continued talking, as the soft wind fanned the fires in the men's pipes. . . .

THE ANIMALS made havoc of the crops. Every night, wild boars, monkeys, and deer came to raid the bananas, the yams, the pineapple, and the maize. Chimpanzees and elephants added to the damage. These animals had learned to avoid the traps that had been set for them.

Large bands of birds infested the rice fields as soon as they were ready for harvesting. And the rodents gnawed everything.

The first to rise and the last to go to bed, Papa N'dabian worked so hard, both in the rain and under the hottest sun, that one day he began to cough.

That morning a man came in from the bush and announced that a panther had carried off a trap. A wounded panther! And this trap had been set on the road that went from the well to the rice fields and the living quarters. Spears, arrows, and guns were brought out. Some men took clubs; others grabbed machetes. Workers from neighbouring camps joined them. . . . And they all set out in search of the wild beast.

Climbié was left behind at the house. Even though it was barricaded, the slightest noise frightened him. Would the thief get away? His heart pounded. A hungry chicken, scratching about for food, pecked at the door, and Climbié froze.

After searching for a long time, the men found the animal lying down in a grove. She sat up as the men approached, tried to spring away, but the chain on the trap held her back. Everyone took cover, the gun-bearers as well as the club-bearers. Then one man, swaggeringly, his arms encircled with good-luck charms, broke away from the others and made his way towards the beast. The animal watched him come. They stared at each other a long time. . . . Walking behind the panther, he seized her tail and twisted it. The beast folded her legs, lay down, and the gun- and club-bearers came to finish her off.

'What happened?' Climbié kept asking himself. 'What power did these good-luck charms have that they could subdue a panther caught in a trap?'

After that day Climbié no longer wanted to go to the well to fetch water, or to the rice fields to eat birds' eggs, or . . . anywhere. Everywhere, he saw panthers. . . .

And each day Papa N'dabian and his wife Bènie discussed this change in Climbié.

'Let him have fun. Later he won't be able to.'

'You spoil this child. How many calabashes has he broken on his way to the well! Look at this bucket he threw on the ground! How many plates do you still have? He has broken them all, one after another.'

'He will change in time.'

'It's now or never. He'll become a nobody, always having fun, running after butterflies, birds, and grasshoppers. . . . Look at all those sores on his feet! If you don't send him to school, what will become of him?'

'Yes, you're right, but who will take this restless child? In the real world you have to know how to read and write in order to be somebody. My younger brother Assouan Koffi is a civil servant. If any Europeans pay me a visit and he isn't with them, we have to talk in sign language, like dumb people, while we grin stupidly at each other. No, the time of ignorance is over now. Today men must understand one another. The children are the future. They must all go to school. I don't want Climbié to suffer the same lot my uncle forced on me. He used to hide me when it came time for school recruitment. Our child must be educated. . . .'

IN MOONLIT DARKNESS, at the first crowing of the cock, Climbié parted once more from the butterflies and the dragon-flies and all the fruit trees, as he left for Grand-Bassam, accompanied by Uncle N'dabian, Aunt Bènie, and

[8]

Cousin Amouzoua. They walked single-file towards the canoe-landing, Uncle N'dabian in the lead. Everything in the dark whispered to him: tree trunks flung across the mud, grass, branches. The frogs croaked, and crickets sang. The water was still and bright, and the hour so hushed that the slightest noise echoed. The mangrove trees jutting over the waterway in wriggling tangles and spilling over in shadowy columns and islets, twisted together and spread apart, huddled in clumps, thrust their points towards the water, then drew themselves far back on the bank. From beneath them came the noise of shellfish and crabs hesitating which direction to go in, of water kissing its old friend the land. The water plashed against the canoe, swaying it with little waves.

Daylight. A rosy sun, which grew larger and climbed the sky, spangling the water with a thousand lights. Barges, islands, schools of fish, the whistle of tugboats. . . . Long after the Eloka ferryboat had passed them, the strongest of all breezes, the sea breeze, brought them the sounds from its helm. After several hours Grand-Bassam was in sight. . . .

The school, encircled by barbed wire and white posts, stood in front of the last house on the way to the beach. In the courtyard was a wash-basin which the students had to fill every morning.

School was reopening! In the morning, very early, children began emerging from all directions, from every corner and alley-way, book-bags under their arms and hoops in their hands. The school, noisy, animated, excited, lived once again. It made one think of the palm trees when the weaver-birds return. The little sparrows had come back. Everywhere singing, shouting, crying. The returning students greeted each other cheerfully, while the newcomers, uprooted from home, looked around for a support. Dropped into a schoolboys' world, bewildered and fidgety, they still clung to their parents.

Nearby some were playing ball or chasing about; elsewhere there were running games and, farther away still, boys were playing leap-frog, blind-man's-buff, and football.

In walked the Headmaster, a big man with an easy stride. At his approach the noise stopped. He acknowledged the many cries of 'Good morning, sir', smiled at everyone, entered the classroom, passed his finger over the blackboard and the bench, put his books on the desk, and seized a switch that had been cut at his request. He bent it; the pliant switch sprang back to its original shape. He tested it on his trousers. The switch was the same size as a walking-stick, but it had the flexibility required of a switch. It did its work well, and was an effective aid in making dull-witted minds learn the elements of French grammar and other subjects.

Switches? Climbié knew all about them. He didn't want to learn any more. He held the writing-slate tightly under his arm and looked at the Headmaster who, standing in the doorway, had just blown his whistle. The students rushed up to him. The experienced ones lined themselves up according to their respective class levels, while the newcomers stood apart. The roll was taken. And each student entered the classroom as his name was called. There were not many new students; the size of the classrooms limited their number. Many parents remained at the door, begging the Headmaster to accept their children, who were crying and refusing to leave.

'There is no more space.'

'They can sit in the aisles, even stand up, just as long as they learn something.'

'Impossible. I already have the maximum number of students.'

'Then what will happen to these children who are turned away from your school?'

'How do you expect me to know?'

'Would they have room at Moossou or Imperial?'

'I don't think so. My colleagues and I are all in the same situation.'

'You can do absolutely nothing for them?'

'Alas!'

And the Headmaster helplessly watched the children leave, because the rule was there, inflexible. The rule is a barrier in the way of life, progress, and the impetuous existence of a society in full evolution. The Headmaster would have gladly enlarged the school with a single gesture. As he stood in the doorway with his outstretched hands straining against the door-frame, he seemed to test it. But the walls would not budge.

The Headmaster watched the parents and their children leave. At the beginning of every school year the same scene occurred, the same sad spectacle. Every year parents would reproach him for not letting their children in. They ignored the rule written on the wall, beside the class time-table.

The wind blew into the classroom in waves, through the large bay windows, rustling the maps, the writing paper, and the books.

'Attention!' shouted the Headmaster, striking the desk with his switch. At the signal, arms crossed and heads rose.

'Stand up, everybody!'

The class stood up.

'One, two, three, four. . . .'

With a loud voice the students sang joyfully, beating out the rhythm with their feet:

> *Students of the countryside,*
> *Let's sing a joyous song.*
> *Soon our books will open wide,*
> *We'll improve ere long,*
> *Yeya!*
> *We'll improve ere long!*

EVERY DAY, slowly but surely, Climbié forgot his origins on a rice plantation, and the thrilling hunts for birds, insects, and butterflies. School assignments, his books, had supplanted the past. To get good marks, to rank high in the class, these were his main concerns now. No other more serious worry touched Climbié, whose life had become one of plenty, happy freedom from care, splendid liberality, and beautiful colours. He laughed hard and played hard, slept soundly, came and went with confidence.

Around Climbié, who had just been given the 'token', Dahoman students mixed with their Eburnean[1] comrades, and swaying their shoulders, sang:

You spoke Fanti,[2] you get the token,
Ha! Ha! You get the token.
You spoke Agni, you get the token,
Ha! Ha! You get the token.

Some of them had hoops and satchels with shoulder-straps, and others carried their books in their hands; all of them, moving in and out, circling about him, blurted in his ears:

You spoke Baoulé, you get the token,
Ha! Ha! You get the token.

The Headmaster stood in the doorway, smiling.

Classes had ended for the day, and outside the school precincts, each student could speak his own dialect. But Climbié, because he had spoken N'zima in the classroom, found himself bearer of the token. He could not get mad; the students dancing and hooting at him were too numerous. His friends took no part in it at all, but the most aggressive among them were probably those on whom he had palmed off the token several times. He watched the students dance around him, then withdraw one by one, as each took the road home.

The little cube was heavy, so heavy, that it forced him to drag his steps. The children departed in happy, noisy, quarrelsome groups. As they drew near, cyclists and motorists beeped and honked their horns ceaselessly.

Climbié returned home alone, abandoned by even his close friends, who were afraid of the token he had in his pocket, along with his marbles and tops.

He ate nothing that noon, he was so worried about getting rid of the little cube. . . . If he still had it at the end of the day, he would have to clean up the courtyard and sweep out all the classrooms, by himself. And the token was at the bottom of his pocket.

Climbié walked along, his head full of ideas, trying to think of the quickest way to rid himself of the little cube, so heavy because of what it symbolized, the lesson it administered.

The token! You don't know what it is! You are lucky. It's a nightmare! It stops you from laughing, feeling alive at school, because everybody is always thinking about it. The bearer of the token – he's the only one people hunt and watch for. Where is it? Doesn't that one over there have it? How about him? The token seems to be under the *pagne*[3] or in the pocket of each student. They all look at each other suspiciously. The token has poisoned the environment, tainted the air, and frozen everyone's heart! You don't know what it is or what lies behind it? Listen: the school inspectors, during their many visits to the schools, often noted the many 'dunces' not wearing caps, and were disturbed by the lax attitude shown towards the language of Vaugelas.[4] Nothing was more painful than hearing the mother-tongue spoken badly, a language heard, learned, from the cradle, a language superior to all others, a little special somehow, a language weighed down with history, and which alone bore witness to the existence of an entire people. The language of France was massacred everywhere: in the schools, in the streets, in the barracks, in the stores. The situation had become intolerable. It was therefore decided to stamp out the evil at its source. The many reports of the inspectors had already emphasized the deficiencies in the teaching of the French language within the primary schools: the students had the annoying habit of always speaking in native dialects, rather than in French.

The collective sabotage of the French language was indeed a terrible thing. Everywhere one heard pidgin versions of a language which is so very refined, airy, and feminine, a language which is like down floating in the breeze or the words a sweetheart whispers in your ear, a language resembling the soft murmur of a madonna, a language which leaves behind it a memory of melody! Instead of this, in the conversations with natives, all along the social ladder from boy to interpreter – with scullion and cook, washerwoman, worker, *garde-cercle*,[5] farmer – one constantly heard such barbarisms as:

[13]

Moi y a dis, lui y a pas content.
Ma commandant, mon femme, ma fils.

And also, words and expressions whose origin you could never hope to find in Littré or Larousse: '*Manigolo . . . Foutou-moi la camp.*'

What sanction could be invoked against individuals who trifled so wantonly with a language as rich, flowing, and diplomatic as French? against those obstinate individuals who never conjugated verbs correctly and who refused to use the time-honoured gender? How many times a day did one hear '*Je partis*' for '*Je pars*', and '*le mangue*' for '*la mangue*'?

It was absolutely imperative to find a cure for this epidemic, so that one might hear '*Mon commandant, il dit que sa femme a accouché*' instead of '*Ma commandant, lui y a dit que son femme il a gagné petit*', or '*Je ne vois pas le Pernod*' instead of '*Moi, y a pas moyen miré Pernod*'. After hearing such language for a while, many Europeans became so thin-skinned, so nervously on edge, that their hands and feet, already fidgety, would fly out of control. One ascribed these sudden fits of anger to the sun or to cockroaches, to solitude, or to the environment. But whatever the cause, whether one thing or another, these spasms came so unexpectedly that people no longer felt safe facing a European. Therefore they took the precaution of drawing back from every advance made by the white man, every advance of a European towards a native – which was hardly a good omen in that heroic age of their relations.

If a European spoke his language correctly, the black man did not understand him. Yet the black man spoke a French so poor that no European understood it. Then the European, to the death of his soul, would try to pidgin-talk his beautiful language, which still the black man did not understand. Finally, nervous and exasperated, angry with himself almost for having brought down his language from the pedestal where other nations had put it, and not knowing which saint, linguist or polyglot, to invoke, he would shout: 'So then, will you never learn to understand French?'

[14]

This distressing situation certainly could not continue. It only caused bitterness on both sides. A remedy had to be found. Hence the decision to outlaw the use of dialects in the primary schools. It was intended in that way, and quickly, to fashion true men, men who would keep true north in all weathers. Well-oriented men, with feet firmly planted in their homeland, but not weathercocks, shifting with the slightest breeze. . . .

The decision was therefore made, and circulars were distributed to all corners of the bush and even to the smallest village schools. 'The speaking of dialects on school property is hereby forbidden.' It was precise. The zones were clearly demarcated. On that day was born the token – a piece of wood, a box of matches, anything. It was entrusted to the top student in the class, whose duty it was to give it immediately to anyone caught speaking his own dialect. From the day the token first appeared, a coldness settled over the school. The students sang as well at the beginning of classes as they did at the end, but without the same abandon, the same gusto, the same fire. And the breaks, once so happy and loud, the breaks waited for impatiently during a lesson poorly understood or when the mind wandered back to an unfinished game of ball, the breaks which reminded one of a bird-cage suddenly thrown open, they too, alas, felt the effects of the new rule. In place of the carefree mingling, the noisy revels and frantic chases, the fights during which dialect was spoken fluently, as if this gave courage, one now saw only small groups of boys whispering timidly, distrusting any person who passed nearby or sat next to them as if by chance. At such times it was always advisable to strike camp. This person would take the liberty of speaking in, say, the Agni dialect; whoever answered him would answer suspiciously in French.

But to a friend, without distrust, you spoke your own dialect. Cheerfully and at once, he would give you the token.

That afternoon Climbié was the first to return to school. Lying down in the sand, he pretended to be asleep. The others returned alone or in small, talkative groups. Climbié was lying in wait for a victim.

What did that one say? There it was! Akrouman, one of the puny little fellows who always hung around Climbié, had just called out in N'zima to one of his friends who was coming through the gate. Climbié, without saying a word, got up and handed him the little cube. The boy jumped back, and Climbié smiled as he ran to play. He could breathe again.

Because of the token the students liked to get as far away as possible from the schoolyard as soon as the final bell rang. They waited anxiously for the time to leave and watched the shadows grow smaller. When the sun reached the twelfth step in the staircase and tried to enter the classroom, they all knew that it was 11.30. Then, without waiting for the schoolmaster to dismiss them, they began to put away their slates, their books, and notebooks. . . .

Uncle N'dabian's cough got worse each day despite the medicines, as many native as European. And each day he also grew thinner; his skin became loose, and his complexion paled. You could now count his ribs. The older people, whispering among themselves, came in and out hurriedly. . . . That evening they were busier than usual. Climbié felt that something strange had happened. He was not mistaken, for just then a woman in tears walked quickly out of the sick-room and said to him: 'Your Papa N'dabian is dead.'

Climbié lowered his head as if in a wind-storm. . . . His uncle, so good to him . . . dead. Never again would they talk together. . . .

That same night the young people built a shelter. Women with bare torsos came wailing and wiping their eyes. Some of them, strips of cotton cloth wrapped around their waists, mourned in muted tones as they retold the entire history of the tribe, the history of this family, and the life-story of the man who had died. The men stayed awake drinking. In the light of the suspended lanterns, the pupils of their eyes flashed blue gleams, the whites of their eyes, their foreheads, and noses glistened, their bald heads were like mirrors. The smoke from the cigarettes and pipes formed a light cloud which the wind carried quickly away.

At dawn Uncle N'dabian, dressed in white, with a handkerchief between his crossed hands, was laid in state on his bed. . . . His face revealed a calm that Climbié had never seen before. Women chased away the flies buzzing around him.

The men talked and drank glass after glass of the gin and rum which the dead man could no longer drink, while the young people with their drums sang and danced. These were the dances that Uncle N'dabian would no longer dance, the songs he would never again sing.

On this day of farewell it seemed as if the men wanted to do all the singing, dancing, and drinking that Uncle N'dabian would have done if he had lived a little longer. But he was lying lifeless on his bed, surrounded by candles constantly flickering in the wind.

Everyone came silently and dropped money in passing.

To all the dancers, the world was only a gigantic cycle of generations, spinning endlessly. For them everything in nature lived. And a man who died, leaving this world for the next, must cross a river on whose bank a boatman kept watch for ever, and must be paid.

Empty bottles accumulated in a corner. Urchins prowled around, ready to steal them and hurry off to sell them.

Towards evening, the body, encased in a coffin and placed on a truck, left for the church and the cemetery, followed by a crowd of people, men and women.

So Death had come and taken his beloved uncle, who used to tell him such beautiful stories. And he had not been able to stop her. Oh, Death is so cruel!

L ITTLE BY LITTLE, life resumed its usual course. Climbié, by grinding hard work, earned admission to the regional school. The school was situated half-way between the military hospital and the civilian prison, at the intersection of Marcel Monnier Street and Lieutenant Welfel Street, near the military camp, which is today the Officers' Mess, and in front of the English firm of Hamilton and Company, exporters of exotic woods.

The school for girls was separated from that of the boys by a hedge of vetivers which the students were unable to cross, though their smiles could, their winks, and signals. The Headmaster, from his landing, often managed to catch them. The punishment then consisted of going to fetch two tubs of manure – cow dung, and blood clots mixed with all the stinking filth of the slaughter-house. The mixture stank so badly that the flies escorted you in your procession from the slaughterhouse to the little garden. For there were two gardens: the little one on the school property itself, and the big one behind the prison. To get to the little garden, you inevitably had to cross in front of that grim-looking wall topped with broken bottles. There was a large gateway. Behind that gate lived prisoners. Often, as the students passed by, the door would open and let a man come out, immediately followed by a *garde-cercle*. The chains around his feet jingled. Every time Climbié passed by there, he looked up at the high moss-covered walls cracked by time, and asked himself: 'What crimes could those men in there have committed?'

To belong to the work-party for the little garden, to water the flower-beds in the company of the girls, was the most ardent wish of every student. Each boy had his own group of girls who brought him water. For nothing in the world would he get water from the well; he preferred water from the pitcher, the pail, or the tub, brought by a graceful young girl. The Headmistress, seeing a boy waiting for his group, a watering-can in his hand, would shout to the girls: 'Bring that water here!' Ah! They would not carry the water like that if the boy did not belong to their group! Lifting the watering-can way up high, the young boys would teasingly sprinkle the girls. The girls, angry, would either empty the water in the alley and walk away, or else fill their hands with water and douse the boys, bursting into laughter. Water came from the right, left, and centre, from everywhere. The boys, watering-can in hand, gave as much in return, but always the girls won, because there were more of them, and they never

[18]

lacked ammunition. But then, what battle does a woman ever lose?

Madame the Headmistress, drawn by all the ringing bursts of laughter, shouted: 'Come! Come! What kind of behaviour is this?'

Silence was restored immediately. Everyone retrieved his pitcher, pail, tub, or watering-can, and the work continued as if it had never been interrupted.

Scenes like these gave charm to the little garden. There, the young girls themselves seemed like large and beautiful flowers; their grace and beauty made the garden grow. And who would not have been charmed by the dashing looks and complexions, the laughter, even the pouting of the young girls of Grand-Bassam, who were talked about as if they were a famous vineyard? And the little kitchen-garden, charmed, would produce much more than the big garden, where lonely men doing forced labour were fighting serious battles, never for fun.

Each boy had his own sweetheart. But Climbié could not decide which girl to choose. He hesitated a long time before making up his mind. And when finally his choice inclined to Nalba, he was in torment. He could never bring himself to speak to her, or even to look her in the eye. Just for her, he made up beautiful sentences in his head, but as soon as she appeared, all the words would get mixed up, then run away, leaving him alone, confused, his head on fire. Nalba's dazzling eyes, her demeanour, the whiteness of her teeth, her eternal smile, her tiny dimples – put his memory to flight, and made him stutter. When his comrades flicked the breasts of the young girls lightly, as if by inadvertence, Climbié envied their boldness, and his heart pounded; but without saying anything, he took the watering-can and began sprinkling the flowers, content solely with her presence, the presence of Nalba.

Climbié did not know how to share in the pleasantries that were thrown out and returned in play, the words which broke the ice and established bridges between the stages of a conquest. He could not make up his mind to utter them, because every time he tried, the young girls murmured smilingly: 'Oh, you too? You, who are so kind, are you going to be like the others?'

[19]

FOR TWO YEARS now there had been little story-books in the supply cupboard. They were meant for the students, but had never been distributed.

One evening after watering, Climbié and his friend Assè found the key on the desk and opened the cupboard. Each one took two books. As soon as Climbié had his in hand, and the cupboard was locked again, his heart began a crazy dance, and his imagination began to work.

He said to himself: 'But this is stealing. They didn't give them to us! That's for sure. And now we've stolen them! I must go to confession, I must tell the priest!' And he did not know where to put the two little story-books, which had, all of a sudden, become very heavy.

'You'll go to prison if the Headmaster finds them in your satchel or in your house. . . .' And the huge, grim-looking wall topped with broken bottles outlined itself before his eyes. The gate opened, only to close savagely behind him. . . . 'And all that for two little books? Why did I take them?'

'It was Assè who gave them to me!' 'That's not true. . . . You have wanted them for several months now. . . . Every time the Headmaster opened the cupboard, you looked at them . . . you devoured them with your eyes. Don't accuse your friend. There's no point in that.' And what resolutions teemed in his overheated brain! Night came, and Climbié tried very hard to sleep. Sleep would not come. He had locked it in the cupboard. Sleep had taken the place of the two little story-books which he held there in his hands. 'Give them back!' 'No! I can't!' . . . 'Well, what are you going to do with them, now that you find them so heavy, so heavy?' . . . 'I wonder . . .' 'Come on, give them back, give them back, I tell you!'

Climbié got up, overcome by this imperious voice, took the two books which were now so heavy, so heavy, and threw them into the classroom through the open shutters.

Sleep, however, did not come to Climbié, for it had taken the place of the two little story-books inside the cupboard.

THE HEADMASTER, because of his rotund body and his long moustache, had been nicknamed *Cabou* by the students. The word made no sense in any of the dialects. But it sounded nice. Every time the Headmaster appeared, the students whispered '*Cabou, Cabou*', without raising their heads, their noses deep in a book or notebook.

One day the Headmaster wanted to get to the bottom of this. He prepared a lecture on the magnifying glass. His paunch was heaving, and his moustache, which he kept pulling and twisting all the time, looked like the tails of a scorpion. The students looked at each other, smiling. Someone breathed the word *Cabou*, which was passed to a third, until it swarmed through the classroom.

'Who are you calling *Cabou*?' asked the Headmaster. A chill passed over the class, and the students lost their smiles. How could anyone explain this word to the Headmaster, who, because he hit so hard, was greatly feared?

But Assè, the most mischievous of the students, without losing his wits, stood up and said:

'In our language, that's what we call a magnifying glass.'

'Ah! You call the magnifying glass *Cabou*!'

'Yes, sir,' replied the students, smiling. '*Cabou!*'

'Well, why are you snickering like that?'

'The name is rather funny,' replied Assè. '*Magnifying glass* sounds better than *Cabou.*'

'*Cabou*, that sounds nice, too. I like it. . . . *Cabou?*'

'Yes, sir, *Cabou!*'

The Headmaster marked the word down in his notebook.

How many scholars must have been misled in the same way as the Headmaster! Then one day, somewhere, he would defend to his death the proposition that the Negroes in the Ivory Coast call the magnifying glass *Cabou*.

WHEN THE STUDENTS left school that afternoon, they learned that a magician had arrived in the city. He was a conjuror, but most people called him a magician because he would come over to you, his hands empty – he showed them to you – and all of a sudden begin pulling coins from your nostrils, serpents from your mouth, banknotes from your hair, and cookies from your pockets. And what was even more marvellous, he told you your past, your present, and predicted your future. Surely now, to manage all that, he must be in communication with spirits. Yet most people called him a magician. Having performed his tricks on the children, in full view of everyone, he jumped into a car and disappeared. Some people even called him a sorcerer. They claimed to have seen him taking part in nocturnal feasts, those banquets of human flesh where women are changed into men and men into women, and where everyone drinks the blood of children from human skulls. A few of them even swore they had seen him at these feasts on such and such a day. Mere boasting, of course, but it was something to worry about. A European sorcerer feasting with African sorcerers!

'What did he look like?'

'He was very tall.'

'What else?'

'He had lots of hair on his head, all over his body, and thick, bushy eyebrows.'

'That's him. . . .'

'And his eyes?'

'You couldn't see them very well, but he must have had the eyes of a white man. That is, they were as clear as a cat's.'

'That's him. . . . That's him. . . .'

'And his voice?'

To tell the truth no one paid much attention to these details. People were at the market-place. The man came there. Many white people often walk around the market-place, and no one noticed this particular one, until, all of a sudden, groups of women and children began scattering in every direction.

'You know how contagious things like this are. . . . It's like being in an ant's nest. Everyone started running. People were shouting everywhere: "A magician! A magician!" We women bolted. . . . A man who comes near you and pulls out of your body whatever he wants to. . . . Then he got into his car and was off.'

'Is he really a man? Don't you think it's a genie who comes to play these tricks?'

'Ah, you never know for sure, but I don't think so. . . .'

'He must be a great sorcerer.'

'Well then? Do you think that white men aren't sorcerers? If they weren't, how could they do so many things? How could they talk long-distance, or fly in the air? Why would they have the eyes of a cat? And the cat is a sorcerer, it divines everything, it speeds the coming of death; and what's more, a cat will flee a house where a man is about to die!'

And from the cat they went on to talk about the dog, and then to tell fabulous stories of ghosts, genies, devils, and sorcerers – all captivating stories which, however, did not let them forget that a magician was in their midst.

The rumour that a magician had arrived spread throughout Grand-Bassam. English subjects, more versed in such matters, said very emphatically that he was a 'conjuror'. But what was a 'conjuror'? This English word had to be explained; examples were cited. And when all this was done, the people would cry out: 'But that's a sorcerer!' For, to succeed in all these feats, you must of necessity be a sorcerer, just like the African sorcerers who made the sun shine and the rain fall at will. Some people had even seen eggs crushed without the shells being so much as cracked; others had seen men who, holding pots of water in their hands, could make the water boil just by blowing on it. How do you explain that? The English subjects became more emphatic than ever. Separating the word into syllables, they insisted: 'He is a con-ju-ror!' Well. . . . Men who held important positions in full view of managing directors and bankers could not all be ignoramuses! There was really nothing to discuss, since these people from the English colonies were certainly men of substance. They had all gone through standard seven and received their diplomas. Some

[23]

had even gone to college. The proof? The proof is that people often went to them to ask their help in drafting a letter to a relative in the Gold Coast. It would be wrong to break the ties with these valuable men over such a silly affair as that of a 'conjuror', a white magician who had just arrived in the city. He was merely a white man who had come to make his fortune, for, as the old people say, if he were truly in communication with spirits, why would he run around the world looking for money, the same money we all look for but never find, the white man's money, which, because it does not understand our language, always eludes us?

But which one of the Whites could he be? All the Eureopeans in Grand-Bassam were known: those in government, those in commerce, and those in the lumbering business. Even their customs and characters were known, as well as the amount of education each had. The entire *curriculum vitae* of each white man was known by every Negro in the city. They suspected nothing, these civilized people who barricaded themselves behind their colour, their white colour erected like a fortress and rampart from which, on high, they watched the Negroes stirring about in their own quarters.

Unable to tot up African society at the end of a day, or even at the end of a month to take account of it all, the Europeans gave all their attention to the coffee, cocoa, rice, copra, cabbage-palm, and lumber, about which they were very well informed, and on whose prices they kept their gaze riveted.

They understood the value of coffee, cocoa, and copra; they visited the stores and carefully examined the full sacks. But they never set foot in the African quarter, whose inhabitants observed the Europeans very closely.

The news of the magician's arrival made the rounds of all the quarters with unbelievable speed. It seemed to have been known at the same moment in Moossou, only four kilometres from the European quarter, at Imperial on the Bingerville road, and in the French quarter. And everyone looked for this magician among all the new faces they encountered. But Mr Magician was invisible. And, moreover, this strange, inexplicable man seemed to know his way around the city amazingly well. In the evening during the cocktail and dinner hours, Climbié and his friends looked for him in front of the hotels and restaurants, but this wicked magician, in order to whet the people's curiosity, remained invisible. Because of this, he became the principal subject of all conversations in the African quarter. All talk began and ended with him.

The villagers from the surrounding countryside brought their produce to market every morning by canoe. They would return home at the end of the day with bits of news, among which was, today, that of the magician. But the farmers had enough on their minds as it was, without worrying about an invisible magician. They preferred to cultivate their lands and keep a close eye on their products, which they could touch, count, and evaluate. So the news of the magician hardly touched them. Among people whose lives were regulated by the day, by the month, by the moon, the stars, the sun, wind, and fog, the news of a magician's arrival could not last long.

In the city these farmers lost their calm manner, confused by the attractions and the noises, but back home in the silence of their farms they found themselves again, were their own masters, and only half listened to you, a stranger, give news of the city. Their thoughts were fixed on the sowing of seeds, an approaching harvest, new fields to plough, traps to visit or set, or on one or the other of their many farm duties. Furthermore, in these villages of endless hard work, of conscious, sustained effort, of continuous struggle, among men for whom every day was a fight against the elements, the news of a magician's arrival could only be turned away. There was no one to give it lodging, to peddle, spread, or plant it. Even the busybodies on their doorsteps talked about other things: pimento, taro, yams, and *pagnes*. For everyone, the news was not good seed. They thought instead of new plantations, of hoeing weeds, of the late rains, of the drop in prices. These were the most important concerns, not the arrival of a white magician. The news was received in the countryside with the same indifference as any other news that was not of immediate value to the work at hand. But in the city, where triviality often prevails over

[25]

level-headedness, the news found choice ground. Indeed, it flourished! Eyes were blinded by the many-coloured signs announcing: 'Tonight at 9.00 sharp, a great performance of prestidigitation.' Prestidigitation. It was a new word for Climbié, who ran to his dictionary to look it up. The dictionary, neutral, said nothing about either magician or 'conjuror'.

The news was rushed to all quarters of the city. There was not a single wall without its cluster of bills, which you read in passing or crowded in front of. There was such a profusion of posters that even the most respectable of walls, that wall on which one never stuck bills, the wall of the Palace of Justice, was flowering with them. A magician was permitted anything! And this one even went as far as defying Dame Justice in her palace! The President stood on his balcony that evening and looked at the signs without saying a word. Was he afraid of the magician, or did the magician have him 'chamé',[6] charmed, in a spell, so that he would not say anything?

And the posters, conscious of their role, of their mission, drew the people's attention, held it, refused to let it go. They were spread out to the right of you, to the left of you, in front of you, and behind you. It was positively raining posters in Grand-Bassam. Masses of papers, thrust about and ripped by the wind, like the wounded in this heroic assault on curiosity, seemed to be dragging themselves to some field-hospital.

Won over by curiosity, people from certain nearby villages came to Grand-Bassam that night, saving any unimportant work for the next day.

The posters had played their role so well that, before the designated hour, the streets adjoining the theatre were full of people, and the auditorium itself was already packed. At the entrance men jostled one another in a crowd that squealed, gesticulated, fought, each wanting to be first. The Bambaras threw their *boubous*[7] over the heads of people; a great lout of a fellow with a Turkish slipper in his hand was beating the head of his neighbour, who held him by the throat; another, with a long walking-stick, tried in vain to force open a way for himself. There was so much pushing and shoving that the *gardes-cercle*, acting as policemen, could not keep the crowd back any longer. The Europeans, the Syrians, and the Senegalese entered through another door, without the slightest scuffle. They stopped there to watch the crowd yelling and fighting one another to see this white magician. The people seemed glued together in a mass. And under the pale moon, some late-comers came running up.

Finally, there he was, our magician, dressed in his long-sleeved black robe, a pointed hat on his head, and a wand in his hand. He climbed on to the stage, bowed, smiled, and thanked everyone with a few clever remarks: 'Honourable assembly, you have come here tonight to see with your own eyes the great miracles man can accomplish provided that he "wants to, knows how to, and dares to!" Daring, ladies and gentlemen, daring is the secret of all success. Willingness is the magic lever of all brilliant performances. I see the willingness, the daring, in every face before me. Watch carefully now!'

He spoke so well and had such a regal bearing! Absolute confidence in himself! He must have had communication with the spirits, for his brightening eyes would emit strange and sudden flashes. At last! There he was before them, their invisible man, their terrible magician, for, already, tales of his exploits had been told throughout the city. Each person, bent on knowing more than his neighbour, had given free rein to his imagination. This man had been seen at the cemetery, enveloped in flames; he had been seen at the seashore talking to Mammy Watta,[8] the siren; he had been seen conversing with spirits. To tell the truth, no one had ever seen him. But what man, in a city which murmurs, chatters, interprets, peddles, amplifies, deforms, and informs, would not assert that he too has some 'late news', is 'up to date'?

People had succeeded in making this ordinary, sleight-of-hand artist into a terrible magician, one, furthermore, who no longer doubted in the least the formidable power that people attributed to him.

The crowd watched him attentively. Each person was determined to be critical. He was a magician, yes, but all the same, no one was going to let himself be deceived! They stared with wide-open eyes, shouting to their comrades in the front rows to watch carefully. They would catch this magician in an ambush of stares! But he continued calmly about his work. From the mouth of a child, he pulled out a long, long, worm. . . . The little boy ran to save himself. The crowd stamped its feet excitedly. Then the magician had a trunk brought out which was pierced with holes; he opened the lid. Inside, nothing. No way out whatsoever. His wife, a pretty little blonde, entered it. The man closed the lid of the trunk after her, and then he began to pass swords through the holes, one by one. The wife screamed, begged. The anguished spectators were witnessing murder. Many people, in their own dialects, shouted at the magician to stop this criminal game. Several women sobbed. The magician laughed, but he calmly continued to thrust the swords, one by one, through the holes.

'Truly, white men have no heart! To kill your own wife, just for money? Doesn't he hear her cries?'

Then, proud of his trick, the magician smiled. A hostile silence filled the room. No one smiled back at him. With an indifference even more insulting to the already indignant audience that was watching, outraged and furious, the magician opened the trunk. His wife? Gone! He shut the trunk again, removed the swords, reopened it, and there she was, the pretty, timid little blonde, walking out of the trunk, smiling. The room breathed hard; hearts started beating again. The prestidigitator was truly a magician!

Finally the 'mystery of the talking skull', which everyone had been waiting for. The magician cleared the table of all his props and covered it entirely with a white cloth. He then placed on the table a platter containing a human skull, a skull with sensational eye-sockets and arches, a skull with all its teeth, a real skull all polished and shining brightly under the electric light. A chill passed through the auditorium. The audience looked respectfully at this skill which had belonged to a man, who most assuredly had suffered long and much, this skull which had fallen so low that it had become a show-piece, a plaything for magicians. The silence was total, profound, heavy, dismal, and oppressive. The polished skull, displayed like this, showed the precariousness of human existence. It belonged to a man who had loved, and who therefore had struggled, who had died, almost certainly, with the sweet and comforting thought that his sacrifice would bring peace and happiness. And this is what he had become. Was this insolent disrespect, this profanation of the dead, a mark of civilization? And the wind which blew into the theatre, engulfing it, brought with it so many sounds! Were the indignant dead rebelling? Were they coming from the depths to take this skull, which was one of their own, away from this foolhardy magician?

'Ladies and gentlemen, this skull you see before you is at your service. You have long believed that the dead cannot speak. But I tell you that the dead do speak, and I will prove it to you. Ask this skull all the questions you want to. Do not be afraid; he will answer you. And this talking skull is only a small part, an infinitesimal manifestation of my power.'

The skull was there on the table, in the platter. It looked even more naked than before. No one spoke. Who would dare be first to ask questions of a human skull, and one which a magician had just struck mercilessly, saying: 'Speak!' Who? Among these men, who would dare overstep the respect due to the dead, even though a whole army of grave-diggers were one day to bury the skull again and pour gin on it to appease the spirits?

Even more important, what respect should not be given to a skull which had housed the thoughts of a man! But the curiosity of one of the spectators was stronger than his beliefs. No one ever knew the author of this profanation, but he must have been from British Africa, because there, with their 'chams',[9] they could afford to be whimsical. This impudent man took his courage in both hands and shouted from the back of the hall:

'Skull, what is your name?'

'Kouadio!'

Ah! It was true that the skull could speak, that the dead do talk! Several good, pious women crossed themselves. You could hear 'Oh, Jesus, Mary, Joseph! What a sin! Making the dead speak!'

Since this impudent man had not been struck dead, the people now felt that they could talk to the skull without fear of repercussions. And all the excited spectators in the auditorium began to

[29]

ask questions. And the naked skull, gleaming under the harsh electric light, answered each person in his own dialect, for it could speak not only Dioula, Baoulé, Agni, and Fanti, but also French and English.

The amazed spectators once again became noisy. Those in the front rows stood up to see better; those in the back rows stood up in turn, telling the people up at the front, not too politely, to sit down again. The front rows pleaded for silence; the back rows kept protesting, and shouted even louder in order to make themselves heard.

The magician was exultant. He walked about looking down at the yelling crowd, rapt with curiosity.

The evening closed with a grand finale. And all those that followed were just as successful. Everyone was anxious to see and question the talking skull.

The young people, as they were leaving, would say: 'It's his boy who answers. His boy is hiding under the table.' No one listened to them. And everybody's imagination went its own way.

Then one fine day the magician disappeared from the city. Tongues and imaginations were unfettered again. Some said one thing, others something else – everybody talked, and what they said would fill volumes.

He had disappeared, leaving his wife in Grand-Bassam, his pretty, timid, blonde wife who always had a chimpanzee following after her. People met her under the mango trees, under the cocoa trees, everywhere that there was a bit of shade and fresh air. She wore the same dress every day. The people could feel that she was unhappy. Since the other Whites never spoke to her, she lived on the edge of the European world. When she passed by, people stared at her strangely, elbowed each other and made rude signs, openly pointed a finger or chin at her, then moved away from her, murmuring: 'She is paying for the recklessness of her husband. The dead are taking their revenge. That's where blasphemy gets you. To be so disrespectful to a man as to dig him up and make him talk! Really now, that's going too far. And you can't go beyond certain limits without asking for punishment. The husband is gone; he's probably dead, and it's the wife who pays.'

'Do you think so?'

'How else can you explain the pitiful situation of the wife of a man who every evening, for weeks, juggled with bundles of money? How could she be so poor, since he showed so much power, if it isn't a curse, a vengeance of the dead? You can laugh. Go ahead. Your laughter won't change the course of things. You see now that one can't play with the dead. They are there, just like tradition. We tell you this, we elders, and you must listen to us. . . .'

But the young people walked away laughing, and the old people called after them:

'Nobody killed Antwi. He killed himself. He is the cause of his own death. It isn't everyone who knows that when it rains one should run into the house.'

CHRISTMAS PASSED, and then came New Year – New Year, with its bands of cheeky boys who swarmed through the streets, wishing 'Happy Holiday' to all comers.

Climbié and his friends each carried a placard which read: 'Happy Holiday! Good Health! Happiness and Long Life!'

They introduced themselves to Europeans, to Africans, to every-one they met. They would run up to somebody and surround him, all of them bawling: 'Happy Holiday, sir! Happy Holiday, sir!' at the same time holding an arm or finger and not letting him pass, until coins, however small, had fallen into their hands. They never dared to go near the *gardes-cercle*, however. For these men only one thing mattered in life: their duty. And 'duty has no play-fellows! For duty is . . . duty.' So, the boys never went up to a *garde-cercle* to wish him well, even on New Year's Day, since in return they would get 'gnons',[10] but not the tasty kind. Moreover, the boys would change path when a *garde-cercle* approached. They were learning discretion.

Climbié loved holidays, not only because of the band contests and the many different dances, but also because on such days the

[31]

foods were different too. Curry sauce, meat-rice, chicken, and European dishes such as green peas, cheese, and biscuits. The boys would fight each other for the last little drop always left in the bottles of syrup and lemonade, chasing each other about, some with a bone in hand, others with a mouthful of food. Really, these holiday meals were a battle. Each youngster wanted to eat more than anyone else of these rare dishes, and he would swallow everything, without even bothering to chew. He had no time to lose. But always, one of the more malicious boys would run away with the dish, and the others would run after him, crying. Often, a youngster unable to keep up with the others would, out of spite, season the food with sand; but it was eaten anyhow. . . .

And if, either at the table or in the kitchen, you somehow managed to get a biscuit or a chicken leg, the first thing to do, to repel the others, was to spit on the food. You could then eat in peace, all alone.

The children were happy, and enjoyed making a game of such tricks. For nothing in the world would they have changed places with the grown-ups who ate without teasing one another, with an unbearably stuffy look. What did anybody need a table and forks for? You ate better with fingers, taking everything from a common plate, laughing all the while.

But all this was nothing compared to the Easter holiday. How impatiently all the children in Grand-Bassam waited for Easter! And for one good reason: the *Yayo*![11]

Before that, however, with the approach of Palm Sunday, they had indulged in date-picking.[12] In the evening, as soon as classes were over, they ran down Azuretti road, throwing their satchels, notebooks, and books aside so that they could more easily run up to the ripened clusters, knocking each other down in their race to reach a tree heavy with dates. They all shouted at the same time, each hurrying to be first: 'It's my tree! I saw it first!' They threw themselves on it, only to take off, almost immediately, and pounce on another tree even richer in fruit. They ran through the brushwood crazily, paying no attention to the sharply pointed leaves or thorns which scratched their feet, legs, hands, and arms. They went on scouring the bush, happily gathering the dates and stuffing themselves with them. They did not feel the sting of the needles in their feet until they started back home, when the pebbles on the road made the thorns hurt. So they sat down and removed the splinters, while overhead the wind murmured in the high grasses. Finally they ran towards the sea in order to soak the dates that were not yet ripe. They ran along the seashore which, night and day, was flogged by angry waves that left behind bits of moss, seaweed, and bubbles tinted many colours by the setting sun.

The sand crabs scurried away at the approach of a wave, gripped the sand a moment so as not to be carried away, then began to scurry off again. Some of them, their heads sticking out of holes, watched this band of prankish boys go by, plunging clusters of dates in the water so as to give them the salty taste people like so much.

But the *Yayo* provided a different sort of pleasure. The *Yayo*! What scenes it brings to mind!

On the Bingerville road, just past the Imperial quarter, there is a bridge. After the bridge, on the left, there used to be the sawmill built by Commander Gros, a very busy sawmill full of machine noises, trucks, and workers. Today it is silent. And at the very site of the mill itself, the sand remains, white and bare.

Two hundred metres from the mill, at a bend in the road, you will find a second bridge under which used to flow a stream of clear, clean water, a little reddish from the laterite in its bed; the women of the quarter used to come there to wash their clothes.

About five metres from this bridge, on the left, there is still a small path: the path of the *Yayo*. How many generations of children in Grand-Bassam have rushed to this spot, have fought one another on this path! How many old people who, when they come to this path, feel happy memories rising in them! And what visions pass before their eyes!

Was it a small path? No! It was an avenue that led to the *Yayos*. A trail through the bush, was it? Wrong, gentlemen. . . . It was a street, the sunniest, the most beautiful, the most animated in the world! Its memory haunts each child for ever. It remains so firmly anchored in him that when he passes it he never fails to look at it with emotion, to smile, with a wistful nod of the head. . . . Ah yes, all that is so long ago! How you would like to be young again, to run down a path once more, to leap over the savannah, bursting with laughter, tumbling against the others, to play even more energetically than you did before. In that way perhaps you could teach children to realize what play is, to enjoy more keenly, to appreciate the good fortune of being a child, the good fortune they bathe in but choose to ignore in their hurry to grow up.

To grow up! Heavens alive! How many men would have liked not to grow up! And who, sighing after joys past and gone, barely enjoy the present!

One afternoon during Holy Week the students, always in undisciplined and noisy groups, would go and fill their pockets with this delicious fruit. It was a mad race between the children from the French, Imperial, and Moossou quarters. Even their frequent scuffles did not stop this race.

They arrived together in the wooded savannah and ran from one bush to another, so fast that some of the boys, smaller or slower than the others, could not manage to get even one piece of fruit. Then – a strange thing perhaps for these combative, egotistical children each of whom just a moment ago wanted to have the most berries possible – they assembled in a clearing near the main road to share their harvest. Then they went on, happy and singing, their hands and pockets full of ammunition, for the war of the mangoes was about to begin.

You knew by looking under the mango trees that the *Yayo*-eaters had been there.

The *gardes-cercle* would give them a good chase. But the children were faster, and easily slipped through their hands and between their legs. The guards, furious, swung their clubs, but the boys always avoided them by careful jumps. Then, turning around, they would boo these guardians of order who no longer remembered their childhood.

In time the boys were organized. There were the 'climbers', the 'gatherers', and the 'watchmen' whose special whistle warned the others of danger. At this signal the 'climbers' would stop dead in the trees, and the 'gatherers' would hide the mangoes in their *pagnes* and walk about with an innocent air, braving the inquisitive and suspicious look of the *gardes-cercle*, a look which went from the mango trees to the children, from the children back to the mango trees, after having taken in all the leaves and branches scattered about on the road. Often, a 'climber', for a joke, dropped a piece of fruit on the head of one of the guards. The guard would run from under the tree to save himself. From a distance he would raise his head to discover the culprit. No one stirred. You did not make fun of a *garde-cercle* without asking for punishment. The boys would scratch their heads, cough, and joke with their neighbours before bursting into laughter.

Sometimes a battle developed between the guards and the children. Caught in a storm of projectiles of all sorts, the guards would beat a hasty retreat, to seek reinforcements. But when they returned, more children! So, everyone left.

The passers-by, especially the foreigners who did not know about the *Yayo*, were astonished when they saw the boys cheerfully eating the green mangoes. These foreigners did not realize that with the *Yayo* even the greenest mangoes lose their sour taste and become temptingly sweet. That is the secret of the *Yayo*.

And for the children of Grand-Bassam, it was, at that time, a tradition, an honour, which they held dear. Never would they have obeyed anyone's order prohibiting them from eating the very first mangoes, the beautiful mangoes whose mere appearance among the leaves made everyone's mouth water.

After indulging in these depradations, the boys, all of a sudden, would run towards the church. On the way, they threw rocks carefully aimed to land on the European houses. Once again they would all disappear before a window opened and the head of a man or woman appeared, looking for the delinquent.

Some would run and fasten themselves on the bells, which, weighed down by all these youngsters, tried calling the faithful to vespers. Others went to sing in the organ loft; and others, with serious faces and candles in their hands, formed a group around the priest at the altar.

c

But all of them, whether they carried hymnbooks or candles, were thinking up new tricks to play on the *gardes-cercle* at the end of vespers.

THERE WAS DANCING every Saturday night, whether at the African Club, the Senegalese Club, or the Dahoman-owned Rose Pavilion. The Rose Pavilion was a fancy place, and all the clerks in government and business frequented it, flocking from Dimbokro, Bouaké, Bingerville, and Aboisso. Throughout the night the streets remained lively. At every intersection an electric light collected the shadows and projected them against the walls, lengthening them and shortening them. Gay lady dancers, their laughs faint and quick, hurried along, leaving in their wakes lingering trails of perfume. The music called out to them, drew them, and they almost ran, so as not to miss a single piece.

How animated the dances at the Rose Pavilion were! The band forgot none of the popular songs, from 'I Have My Own Scheme' and 'Under the Bridges of Paris' to 'China Night'.

The waltz and the tango were not very popular. Only those dancers who wanted to show off their talent asked for them. On the other hand, as soon as the first notes of a march were sounded, everyone sprang to his feet, as if propelled by a piece of elastic, to fight over the lady dancers. A veritable donnybrook.

'Pardon me!'

'That's all right.'

'*Pouèt-pouèt! Pouèt-pouèt!*' the dancers would shout, shuffling and gyrating. As soon as an opening appeared, everyone hurried in that direction. A few big fellows, to break loose from the crowd, would dance roughly. And this frequently caused a brawl. But it was only an interlude. The proprietor would make the 'boxers' leave, and the dance would continue. Everyone swayed to the rhythm of the music, clinging to one another, perspiring. And if a certain rendition happened to please them more than the others, the band would play it longer, and the men would dance as long as it played. If the exhausted musicians stopped, the dancers and spectators shouted with one voice: 'More! More! We paid to dance!' And so, dancing there had to be. The spectators outside the building jumped up, their head-dresses bobbing in the air, and cried at the top of their voices: 'More! More!' And when the piece was begun again, they grabbed their partners and danced, free of charge. But the joy of dancing would not reach its peak until the cornet, with a few quick notes, announced a *pathy*, a traditional song, or an *agbass*, a dance of their homeland. People now danced singly, each yielding to the impulses of his heart and spirit, as if to stamp out all worries, present and future. Everyone sang. The band could go away, but the people would dance anyhow. Openly, everyone pulled out his handkerchief to wipe off the sweat, for it was hot, despite the nearness of the lagoon reflecting all the lights.

In the African quarter other bands brought men, women, and children dancing out into the open air.

The Paris Bar and the France Hotel, for their part, entertained the Europeans with gala soirées given by performers from France or Dakar. These performers more often than not had a Negro accordionist or violinist accompanying them. The Africans, therefore, would run to these hotels to see the spectacle of one of their own people playing with a group of Europeans. These musicians came from Dahomey. Their proud compatriots kept inviting them out and would never stop talking about the progress of Dahomey, the newspapers of Dahomey, the lawyers of Dahomey, the novelists of Dahomey.

They were determined to vaunt the progress of their country by comparing it to the 'primitiveness' of the Ivory Coast, whose inhabitants were still dazzled by the brilliance of European civilization. They talked about it so much that, in time, relations became strained, and even more strained as the Dahomans gradually occupied the highest official positions and filled other posts with their relations, while native office-holders were being dispossessed.

The day after these grand soirées, where the champagne flowed freely at the tables of lumbermen and garage-men, Climbié and the other children of the quarter would go and collect the paper streamers, the balloons, and empty biscuit boxes which servants in shirt-sleeves and rolled-up trousers swept into the streets.

On Sunday mornings the church was filled with the faithful, but very few Whites were there.

The Europeans, tired of reciting 'Our Father Who Art In Heaven, Give Us Our Daily Bread', had without a doubt either decided to get this bread without the help of the 'Father', or, simply satiated, preferred to sleep all morning. Their slogan seemed to be: 'God helps those who help themselves.'

Monday came again. Very early in the morning the siren on the wharf gave the signal to begin work.

The Khorogos,[13] lumber haulers, got up very early to harness themselves in their ropes. They chanted, and the lines of tip-wagons seemed to move on their own. No one noticed the bulging muscles, the straining of bent knees, the feet scraping the ground. The Fanti and Sierra Leonean coopers, in the service of powerful commercial societies, danced to the sound of their own music around the barrels they were repairing. They were grouped in teams of two, three, and four. From morning to night during a working day, Grand-Bassam filled with music, and all the going and coming in the city seemed to move in rhythm.

The market-place teemed with people. Customers moved along the narrow passageways between the stalls. They could barely stop to bargain. They had to keep walking in the wave of people which surged past the pedlars of sugar bread, jewellery, handkerchiefs, and *pagnes*, the sellers of fish and seasonings, the butcher's stall with its smell of fresh blood. . . .

The traders quarrelled over the customers, good-naturedly. It was up to whoever could hawk his merchandise the best to draw in a customer, keep hold of him, and force his hand.

Throwing their satchels over their shoulders, Climbié and his friends would leave for school, a slice of bread-and-butter in their hands, a bite in their mouths. They too stocked up with supplies from the market-place, teasing the schoolgirls as they left.

One morning the 'cinema' came to town on a truck. The news

spread immediately through the living quarters and the shopping area.

The nights the movies were shown were indeed like holidays. To draw a crowd musicians were hired, and since they were entitled to free seats for the performance, they played the role of beater with gusto. They followed behind two boys who carried the programme.

The performances took place either in the public market-place, or on the sand in the French quarter at the intersection of Commandant Pineau Street and Bouvet Street.

The presence of attendants posted around the tarpaulin-covered fence did not prevent the many gate-crashers from raising the tarpaulins and entering without paying. During the interval the guards fell sound asleep at the ticket gate and snored loudly, awakening at the start of the second half of the show.

Everywhere round about, sly fellows perched in trees or stood on barrels to see the film.

Sometimes it would suddenly start raining. The performance then became a free-for-all, and the show ended abruptly. Often the projector threatened to catch fire, and this meant another quick exit.

During evening hours couples would stroll along the streets. They walked slowly, their arms twined around each other's waists, breathing in deeply the cool breeze of the lagoon. Softly they sang:

> *Ehoulé m'ba hou ihôn ya hô!*
> *Ehoulé m'ba hou ihôn ya hô, mamin Amah*
> *Tidi n'dètrè gba min so hô.*[14]

Women and young girls stood in front of jewellery stalls, waiting for the delivery of a jewel promised to them for over a year. But the jeweller's apprentices, in collusion with their superiors, just laughed, and with a lamp in one hand and a hammer in the other, they said to their customers: 'The owner is not here.'

'Where is he?'

'He's in Grand-Lahou.'

'When will he be back?'

'We don't know.'

'A downright liar!' In our country one could just as easily have said: 'He lies like a jeweller.'

Men would gather under the Cayenne almond trees to play ball or cards. Old men from Senegal, dressed in long *boubous*, walking-sticks between their knees, would lie in lounge chairs near by and talk about the time in their youth when they first set foot on the Ivory Coast. They had never gone back to their native land, and now they had almost no teeth, and their hair was as white as their starched *boubous* draped over the chairs.

The cargo boats, dirty and coal-black, never stopped gulping in the products brought to them by whale-boats. Wooden rafts were hoisted on deck by the winches, and then made to disappear in their iron bellies. The hungry, black cargo boats, and they were always there, kept craving other foods, other products: oil, palm-cabbage, cocoa, and coffee. Then one morning they pulled anchor and mournfully went out to sea, spitting black smoke as if wanting to blur their passage.

Every two weeks the *Canada*, the *Madonna*, the *Brazza*, the *Touareg*, the *Hoggar*, and the *Asia* dropped anchor in the port, bringing packages and passengers: colonists, functionaries, and young people seeking work or a quick fortune.

The shops were very well stocked. The people from the neighbouring villages of Alépé, Bonoua, Ebra, and Adiéké came to sell their products and buy in a supply of tobacco, soap, sugar, petrol, oil, matches, liquor, perfume, and tools.

Money flowed easily from pockets, from the lining of hats where the old people would hide it, from under the edge of *pagnes* where the women sewed it. The shop windows displayed *pagnes* in all colours and designs, silk scarves in brilliant hues, perfumes of all kinds, and drinks of all flavours and all strengths. The liquor department was the busiest and the noisiest. Gin and rum were carried away by the caseful, and could also be consumed on the spot, in a corner of this vast department. Men stayed to discuss the day's events over drinks and would empty whole bottles of these noxious liquids. Many left the place happy, light-headed, staggering a bit, and sputtering continually. What did this matter to the European who made a profit from gin and rum? First their smell intoxicates, then the taste burns your tongue a little, scrapes your throat, and sets your chest on fire. This flame runs throughout your whole body; it shakes you and makes you wobble, as if wanting to spill all your worries to the floor before taking you to the point where you forget the present.

On the counter in every shop was a Roberval scale, used to weigh small quantities: black leaf tobacco, bulk sugar, marine salt, rock salt, pimento, pepper, onion, and dry fish. Through the doorway the scent of all these products, mixed with tar, naphthaline, various oils, and smells of all kinds, assaulted you, thronged round you, clung to you, each attracting you in its own way.

At the entrance you could buy coffee, palm-cabbage, cocoa, and palm-oil. And so the shops, whose role was to make money circulate, gave it out with one hand and took it back with the other. It is certainly safer under lock and key than tucked under the lining of a hat or sewn under the edge of a *pagne*. Money is entitled to a certain respect, anyhow.

And every day the cargo boats dropped anchor and vomited their loads on the land: pots, buckets, dishes, lamps, knives, machetes, glass trinkets, cigarettes, bundles of cloth, cement, building materials, pipes, preserves, cases of liquor, barrels of wine, a little bit of everything that the factories of America and Europe feverishly produced night and day at an ever-faster pace.

Periwinkle, bougainvillea, oleander, canna, pride-of-China, and cockscomb bloomed all along the white fences. . . . Cats rolled up like balls slept on window-sills, while the wind, together with the birds, never stopped whistling in the cocoa trees.

The people of Grand-Bassam worked earnestly and lived peacefully, the Europeans on one side, the Africans on the other.

On some days the Europeans or the Africans would escort one of their own to his last resting-place. The dead man's dreams and illusions, exhaled with his last breath, had killed him, and they remained there, in the air, to add their weight to the weight of other men's dreams and illusions. For they would never allow themselves to be buried.

The Europeans accompanied their 'brother' in silent cortège;

the Africans their 'relative' in a noisy, hymn-singing crowd. Sometimes, depending on the importance of a person, a fanfare of drums led the procession.

Standing on the front steps of shops or behind the counters, Europeans watched the passing crowd of men, women, and children who sang and chattered at the same time.

Always, a European motorist, hurrying to a business appointment, would cross in front of the crowd at full speed, as if suddenly he had the desire to behave badly, to dispense with manners, or to show off in front of other Europeans. Others, on the contrary, saluted and crossed themselves. The dead man had no colour any more. He was no longer of our world, once he had been relieved of his fears and his rebellious spirit. He was a lesson to all those walking behind him, for he placed the happy and the unhappy in their proper perspective. The dead man passed by the Europeans, and for a long time they remained there, saluting and thinking. Then they put their hats back on again and went their way, that is to say, with their dreams and illusions. Do they too think that life is only a dance before the final sleep? . . .

Such was life in Grand-Bassam, until, one evening, the news of the sudden death of the Police Commissioner broke over the city.

'The Police Commissioner is dead!'

'That's what people are saying.'

'What happened?'

'No one knows yet.'

'Was it suicide? Did he drown?'

'No one knows anything.'

'What does the doctor say?'

'He went to examine the body, but he has said nothing yet.'

'He must have killed himself. . . . The Europeans, you know, often put a revolver to their heads! . . . What about his wife? And his children?'

'They are with him.'

'Are they wounded?'

'No!'

'Then we can't talk of suicide. . . . Do you remember that noon, on the balcony of one of those important houses, when we heard gunshots – bang! bang! – followed by shouts, footsteps, and sobs? A young European, after having shot his wife and children, ended up by shooting himself.'

'They have everything, and they go and kill themselves. Well now, what are we supposed to do, we who are less well off?'

'That is perhaps one of the main reasons why Africans aren't allowed to have guns. But the Police Commissioner, was he sick? Since when?'

The details were slowly pieced together. The Commissioner of Police had been confined to bed for two days. The doctor called to his bedside had written out many prescriptions. He had whispered something to the wife who, all during the examination, kept questioning the doctor with an intense look. The doctor never once wrinkled his brow or dropped his arms to his side despairingly. He still had hope. But in the official household the phones had not stopped ringing after his visit.

And then, the awful, last detail: the sick man had vomited.

The news went everywhere, buffeting the city. The Africans knew well that they would share in the grief of the Europeans, because, as always in such circumstances, they were forbidden to dance in their quarter at night.

The terrible news stirred everything in its passage. It rustled the thatched roofs, entered the small huts, bringing old women to their doorsteps, and awakened drowsy men lying in the sand.

'Ah, these Whites! Do you remember the story about the cashier, the one about the lumberman, and. . . . Will we never stop telling stories about disillusioned Whites who kill themselves in Africa? Because a fiancée hasn't answered a letter, bang! someone kills himself. Because money is missing from the cashbox, bang! someone kills himself.

'They brought their prison with them. They are afraid of it, yet they throw us in it under the slightest pretext.

'Listen. One day some friends and I were sleeping under a covered walk-way. You weren't born yet, you others. Suddenly we heard noise around us. We woke up with a start, and who did we see? The Commandant and his guards.

' "What do you do?" the white man asked us.

' "We are fishermen."

' "And what are you doing now?"

' "We are doing nothing. We are sleeping for the moment."

' "No, you're loitering. . . . Where are your permits?"

'We didn't have them on us, and he gave each of us fifteen days in prison. All the time we were there we kept asking ourselves: "Did the Commandant put us in prison because we didn't have our permits, or was it because we were sleeping?" '

News about the Police Commissioner continued to come, calling forth memories in the white heads of the old men. And it was now clear.

The Commissioner of Police had vomited! . . . It was Negro vomit, yellow fever, the terrible and pitiless yellow fever, the terror of the European colony. That was the reason for the many telephone calls between the doctor and the *Commandant de Cercle*.[15] That same night prudent Europeans left for Abidjan. The next morning a quarantine was declared. Boats kept to the open sea, crowds were prohibited, dances were suppressed, there was an obligatory curfew at 8.00. Grand-Bassam took on a strange look. At sunset the Europeans drew on their gloves, put on their boots, and veiled themselves. No more catechism, no more choir practice, at the close of which Climbié and the other children used to fill the streets with shouting, singing, and laughter. They no longer chased the young girls, who ran away laughing. No longer were they able to catch and pinch them here, pinch them there . . . then, satisfied, let the girls go on their way, grumbling, but happy none the less to have been pinched here and pinched there.

All that was finished for the moment, because the Police Commissioner had vomited before dying. Troops of sanitary police swept through the city, seeking out the bottles and empty boxes lying around. Stagnant ponds were filled in. Every day more inhabitants were vaccinated.

The Europeans lived in a state of anxiety. The smallest insect on the wall made them jump. Gramophones were silent. Music would surely call out the insects, 'whose manners it could never hope to sweeten!'

The Africans wore no veils and continued to sleep under the stars because it was too hot in the huts. The mosquitoes buzzed in their ears, stole a little blood, and then flew elsewhere if they were not crushed for having bitten their victims too hard.

Frequently several Africans died at the same time, but it was not Negro vomit. For when it came to these deaths, other causes were always found. . . . How many men, before the death of the Police Commissioner, had vomited before dying?

Often in the French quarter, during the evening hours, a drum revolted against the strict quarantine and threw out high-pitched notes into the young night, while the Europeans were drawing on their gloves, putting on their boots, and veiling themselves.

And the beat of this drum was the plea of Grand-Bassam, the Bassam of dances, which seemed to call out to the Europeans always ready to slip under their mosquito nets:

> *Give us back our songs!*
> *Give us back our dances!*

IN NOISY, quarrelsome groups, the students would start out for school, playing ball along the way. One day a car hit one of them and injured him. The others stopped playing for a moment, only to begin again even more enthusiastically. Parents would search their children for the balls, but in vain; they were hidden in the sand at the foot of a wall or a tree before the children came home.

The cyclists and motorists would sound their horns to no avail, and climb down angrily from their vehicles. Once a young cyclist shouted at the students menacingly:

'You kids there, you dirties! Ain't you heard the horns? Balls, always balls! Balls, you eat 'em too?'

After that, crude replies flew out of every mouth, from all sides of the street. The children would all come running up whenever an older student confronted them. The solidarity of youngsters before older people – all the gesticulating, the glittering eyes, the

[45]

jumbled voices! Then the children separated, to regroup a little farther on, because the cyclist had threatened them, and an old man, coming from the direction of the school, had grabbed a few of them by the neck. They scampered away as fast as their legs could carry them, since it was time for class.

Climbié no longer played ball, however. He would linger in front of S.A.C.O., a bookshop, the only one painfully trying to exist in the midst of all the important establishments in the area: the C.F.A.O., S.C.O.A., C.I.C.A., C.F.C.I., C.R.O.A,,[16] Woodin and Périnaud, which the Africans called Pozzo di Borgo, the Soucail, and the French Company of Kong, which was persistently called Nvéridjé after its founder Verdier.[17]

Climbié would stare at the books with their illustrated covers and colourful titles. His eyes went from counter to counter, devouring them all. There was every type of book, from the most serious novel to the most vulgar detective story, from the occult sciences to mathematics, from simple grammar books to philosophy textbooks, and this did not include the magazines. There were books everywhere: on shelves, on counters, in boxes, on top of crates, in stacks, or spread out. And their colours blended so well that they would catch your eye, draw you in, then hold you fascinated. You were seduced, charmed, and bewitched, and you would enter the bookstore whether you wanted to or not. Climbié and his friends Dibetchi and N'da would spend most of their time there. Dibetchi, the wealthiest of the threesome, always bought a new wild-west adventure story. Each would take his turn admiring it, and their conversations were sprinkled with expressions like: 'Signor Caballero! Amigo! Bona dios!' Each one lived with his favourite hero, speaking in Spanish, no longer in French. Did they miss anything? Cowboy hats, revolvers, cowboy pants, horses? No, of course not. The habit does not make the monk.

That evening Climbié was engrossed in one of these books when his uncle Assouan Koffi called him. His heart skipped a beat. What had he done now? Within a few seconds he had accounted for all his actions. No, today he had not done anything to be ashamed of. No broken dishes; his bed was made, the table cleared and wiped clean. Reassured, he presented himself. His uncle was slowly leafing through an illustrated book.

'Look at these photos,' he said. 'Come here. . . . Stand over here, at my right, so you can see better.'

And the pages were turned, one by one. Climbié looked at the photographs. Wait, a man in handcuffs, surrounded by white policemen.

'Did he steal something?'

'No. . . .'

'What did he do then?'

'He was fighting for his fellow Negroes, who are unhappy.'

'Where did it happen?'

'Oh, very far from here, in Harlem, in America. This man had been saying things like "Africa for Africans".'

'Is what he said not good?'

'Well, some people believe that he had no business doing what he did, or advancing such ideas.'

'Why is that?'

'Because of their self-interest, that is to say, their own safety. . . .'

Climbié did not understand all this. What struck him was that this well-dressed Negro was in handcuffs and being escorted down a main street, where the people passing by did not even notice what was going on around them.

On another page, Whites were bludgeoning a crowd. Whites beating other Whites, just the way Negroes are beaten. What did all this mean? . . .

'Where do they sell this book?'

'It isn't for sale. If anybody saw it in my hands, I'd be thrown into prison.'

'Are there books then that people shouldn't read?'

'As far as I'm concerned, you should read everything, and that's why I was anxious to show this book to you.'

'I just don't understand all this.'

'You will understand, my child, later on. For the moment you have only one job, to study. Your studies will teach you to help every man who is suffering, for he's your brother. Never look at a man's colour; it doesn't mean a thing. But, on the other hand, don't ever let anybody step on your rights as a man, for even in the worst slavery, those rights are part of your very nature. Today Europeans show their teeth, beat you and kick you. Before, my father told me, when you greeted them, they stopped and took an interest in you, in your wife and children, and always asked: "How are you?" And the old people would answer: "Thank you, thank you!" They shook your hand, and when they left they smiled, pinched your child's cheek, and slipped a few pennies in his hand. They had hearts then. They were human and closer to us, by far. But in our day the Europeans no longer have the time, and when you greet them they hardly look at you, and even the kindest of them just say: "All right, all right," as they hurry after money. Some of them, though, come down to our level, take an interest in us. A few have learned to get acquainted with the heart, and to understand it before running after money. Others, on the contrary, feel compelled to run after money, which is what they have left their countries for, before even glancing at people of such a different colour. But why, when they come to write about the Black world, those people, why do they only come out with works in an exotic style?

'Europe has a queer optical illusion about Africa and its people. The originality of Africa? A naked man. Its genius? A woman with lips like platters. Why do they insist on popularizing such an over-simplified view of Black Africa? Are they telling us to go back to our origins, not to let outselves be uprooted, to hang on to our traditions?

'A naked man! A woman with deformed lips!

'The painful effort of an entire people slowly changing their customs, casting away their foundations, the convulsive gasps of a spirit, choking and fighting, the constant, never-ending struggle with yourself, with the past, with the present, with the old people, with everything – no, that doesn't count.

'A buyer of black monkey-skins, nourished on the theory of evolution, and Cartesian to boot, the European is truly convinced that, in the evolution of the human species, after the monkey, man became black, then red, then yellow, and finally white. The colour white is thus for him the test of a civilized man.

'He is convinced that no one would know how to get along without him, that on this continent happiness, constantly hunted down, would never know where to take shelter. . . .

' "All right, all right," say the kindest of them as they run after money. . . .'

A RELIGIOUS ATMOSPHERE had settled over the school with the approach of final exams. Every day the students would talk about Novenas, the three Ave Marias; they prayed to Saint Teresa, to the baby Jesus, and to Saint Joseph.

Climbié and his friends, having become true pillars of the church, did not lift their noses out of their geography books, their books of natural history and French history, except to immerse themselves in their hymnals.

All games had stopped. There was a single obsession: to pass the exams. Instead of fighting each other under the mango trees after classes, they retired in small groups, books and notebooks in hand, and asked each other questions.

Then came the happy outcome and entrance into the *Ecole Primaire Supérieure*, the E.P.S.

Sunday night, the night before he was to leave, Climbié did not sleep a wink. At last he was going to the E.P.S.! For a long time now these three letters had drawn him like a lover. If he had worked so hard, had taken so many communions, had recited so many prayers at the approach of the exams, it was so as to enter the E.P.S. If he had never rebelled against the many punishments inflicted on him, most of them truly absurd, it was to be able to go to the E.P.S.

The E.P.S.! You have no idea what it meant to the students, and what a bugbear it became at the hands of the Headmaster! For all, or nothing at all, he had only one refrain: 'You there, you won't go to the E.P.S.!' For, in order to be admitted, good conduct counted as much, if not more, than pass marks. To pass the exams, some students had become so well-behaved that, if they

[49]

had died in class or on the school grounds, they probably would have gone straight to heaven. Several, however, ended up kicking over the traces. Postponing their certificates of study and the E.P.S. until a later date, they packed their bags and left. Many succeeded in getting themselves hired as civil servants, writing occasionally, then styling themselves 'writers', eager to designate all the 'leading writers', far above their class, as candidates for retirement.

Climbié was going to enter the E.P.S. But he no longer wanted to leave Grand-Bassam, which belonged to every fibre of his being. Never until this night had he known how much he loved this city, how much he was a part of it, how deeply rooted this city was in him. Happy memories once again rose to his mind: the choir practices, the games after catechism, the *Yayo*, fishing, swimming in the lagoon, the young girls he used to tease; everything in him this night had taken on a strange perspective. He found a charm in the monotonous drone of the ocean. Jealous Grand-Bassam was determined to hold to her breast all the boys she had given birth to and reared, who breathed her healthy air. Climbié would have liked to leave with Grand-Bassam at his side, with all the young girls who had brought him pitchers of water, with Nalba, whose mere sight or presence made him feel empty-headed.

Finally, Climbié was a *groupéen*.[18] He had just weathered a cape in the voyage of his studies. He would steam from bay to bay towards the *Ecole Normale William Ponty de Gorée*, the large Federal school.

He could not sleep, so many projects multiplied and jogged around in his head. He would finally be able to help his mother. What type of work would enable him to make her happy? I'll find that out at the E.P.S., he said to himself as he stared at his suitcase. . . .

Morning came at last. A morning which seemed to be unlike any other, a morning when all one's feelings were skin-deep.

It was a Monday at the end of September. Climbié was the first passenger to arrive at the wharf. The launch would not leave until 7.00. He knew that, of course. But that night he had made a decision: 'to forget child's play and buckle down to work', a resolution which already he was putting into practice by proceeding to the wharf at 5.00, his heavy suitcase on his shoulder.

Grand-Bassam said nothing more to him. The ties between them were broken. The magic was gone now, and in its place was his determination to leave, quickly, and go down there, to Bingerville, to be in the *Groupe Scolaire Central* at the *Ecole Primaire Supérieure*, to pass the competitive exams for entrance into the *Ecole William Ponty*.

He forgot his girl friends, that is, Nalba, and was even a little angry with himself for having wished the vacation longer because it was fun. A voice had cried out to him: 'And your mother then? Are you going to forget her?' That broke the spell.

Climbié did not know his mother very well, since he had been separated from her very young. Had he ever known a mother's caresses? All he remembered was that she never beat him, since he was her only surviving child.

Whenever the ocean was stormy, his mother would always keep a close eye on him, for he loved to go and look at the seaweed, to catch the crabs stunned by the surf, to collect the conch shells which the waves brought in from far away. Grabbing him by the arms, she would say: 'Stay here!' He would stay, but as soon as his mother's attention was diverted, he would once again take off after the crabs and shells. She would come after him, saying: 'Are your ears stopped up? Don't you listen to anything anyone tells you? Don't you see that the ocean is stormy, that it's looking for men to snatch up, to eat them? When the ocean shouts like that, it's hungry. Don't you know that?'

Then, Climbié would stay close beside his mother. He would watch her peel bananas and poke the fire, while the chickens fluttered around her, pecking at the skins.

He must finish school quickly so that he could take care of his mother. You could have girl friends by the dozen, but you only have one mother.

The other students, all very well-dressed, arrived in cheerful groups. Girl friends and parents accompanied them. Climbié, however, was alone. He kept out of the way of all the noise and laughter. Each sound, each laugh, said to him: 'Work! Work! Hurry up and finish school!'

The old people all gave the same advice: 'Work hard. Be polite, obedient, and attentive. Don't let them send you home because of some foolish prank. We are all counting on you. So work hard. And most important, don't think about girls. You are young. You have plenty of time for that later. For the time being, you must study. You will reap only what you sow. And don't forget that "a broken leg can still take another step", that "even a dead lion is more frightening than a lamb". Think always of these proverbs, for we will no longer be near by to advise you. Learn how to conduct yourselves. Ignorant people have no place in the real world. The learned man is a lion. Learn all you can, but don't abandon your customs.'

The children listened distractedly to this old advice from the old people. For they kept their eyes on their girl friends, who were motioning them to come.

Ah, it was truly an event, the departure of the students for the 'group'! Everyone was eager to give them a present. From the market-place, the women brought cartons of bread-and-butter, nuts, rice-cakes, and fritters, placed in dishes and tied up with beautiful cloths. People came running up from the shops near by, carrying tins of preserves, pilchards, sardines, tunny fish, corned beef, cheese, bread, packages of sugar, boxes of cookies, bottles of wine. . . . Noise rose from everywhere: from the market-place, from the shops, from the wharf. Climbié remained alone. As he looked at the mothers of his friends, he thought of his own, whom he scarcely knew, but remembered no feature so prominent that he could say: 'My mother is this tall, and this big.' She was blind in one eye. But which eye? He just did not know. And more terrible still, she did not want Climbié to come and see her lest he also die from the mysterious evil that had cruelly killed her three other children at the age of four. They had gone to bed one evening, and in the morning were found dead. The family accused the grandmother of having promised them to the sorcerers for their nocturnal feasts.

Nevertheless, Climbié had rounded the cape of tragedy without difficulty. But his mother was not reassured, and that was why, after sending her son away from the village, she wanted him never to set foot there again, at any cost.

The dock-workers loaded the launch with tanks of petrol, barrels of oil and liquor, bales of cloth, cases of tobacco, and mail sacks.

One by one the passengers climbed aboard. One, two, three bursts of the siren. The third, the longest, made up of successive blasts, more or less short, droned up and down the entire scale. Everyone in Grand-Bassam knew what the third whistle meant. It was the warning to late-comers. One would always see them running up, dashing headlong through the crowd, barely shaking the hands extended towards them, forgetting to grab a package, then jumping on to the launch, puffing loudly as if to say: 'I was lucky!'

That day, however, there were no late arrivals. And as soon as the signal to leave was given, everywhere on the wharf parents were embracing their children tearfully and pronouncing their blessings in loud voices.

Nalba was there. Though he wanted to desperately, Climbié did not have the courage to shake her hand, much less to kiss her. Almost immediately he thought of his mother, and the idea of buckling down to work eliminated all other thoughts.

The time for departure had finally come. The launch pulled away from the wharf slowly, as if wanting to draw out the people's emotions, to break them delicately. The pilot seemed willing to prolong the emotional farewells. The engine bells kept ringing, while hands and handkerchiefs waved good-bye. People were shouting to one another: '*Bon voyage!* See you soon! See you Christmas!'

The students knew that it would be the Christmas and New Year vacation before they would have the chance to return to their native land, in the uniform of a *groupéen*, a simple khaki outfit with a short collar, a blue cap with a black peak, and white linen shoes with rubber soles. This khaki outfit was made by the nuns of Moossou, and the measurements taken from young girls who were already fully developed. That is why the front of the jacket bulged a little too much on the young male chests. The boy students at the *Ecole Primaire Supérieure de Bingerville* did not have the pretty breasts of the beautiful young girls at the *Institution Notre-Dame des Apôtres*! But that made no difference. They belonged to the 'group'. And they strutted about like peacocks.

The launch travelled on. It passed in front of the banana market where women were battling with the *gardes-cercle*, arguing about who would be served first. Nothing could be heard but their cries, their pleas, their shouts, and curses. The *gardes-cercle* drove them back. The women charged forward again. The guards' clubs reared over their heads, then fell on the mass of women who refused to budge. Armed with buckets full of water, the guards doused them. But the women were determined to have their bananas and fish. A husband, when he returns home, must find something to keep him going. These women are the heroines of the prosaic struggle for life.

The launch whistled with all its might. The women did not even turn their heads.

One by one the shops and houses glided by; people on the shore passed in succession; trees and electric wires ran together, then disappeared.

Petit-Paris could be seen through the leaves of the cocoa and mango trees; Imperial followed, with its telephone poles, its white lighthouse, and its many small shacks.

Finally Moossou appeared, and men could be seen repairing nets, and women buying yams and fish without even the slightest scuffle. Children, fishing or swimming, shouted greetings at the travellers. The more courageous ones swam towards the launch. When they were tired of the chase, they dived down, then floated on their backs, spitting streams of water into the air.

The launch rounded a bend in the river, and the houses disappeared. . . . Colourful birds darted in and out of mangroves and other trees caressed by ferns. Over here a gulf, over there a peninsula, a little farther on an island, and always the forest on both banks, with camp sites appearing now and then. And schools of fish, and fishermen alone or in small groups. And motorboats straining to pull long lines of barges loaded down with canvas-covered merchandise, with a man standing at the helm, watching. And wooden rafts heading towards Grand-Bassam. Giant trees on both banks, some bare, others bushy, mangroves encrusted with shellfish, umbrella trees with white trunks, flowering bushes, palm trees with creepers tangled about their branches, and leaves of all colours, from the rosiest pink to the deepest yellow. And on all this the sun cast its fiery rays.

On board the launch, the happy students were singing. They were all dreaming of the beautiful life awaiting them. Not yet having lived out the present, the future worried them but little. They saw glimpses of it in the smiles of their girl friends, in their bubbling youthfulness, whose overflow spilled forth in peals of laughter, in songs learned by heart. In everyone they met, passed by, or talked to – clerks, dock-workers, farmers, labourers – they saw only the exterior. They ignored the drama of their everyday existence. At this age, what could they really know about life? They just sang.

Several of them began eating the roasted chicken and the other dishes which had been lovingly prepared for them. The arrangement of the plates, the colours of the bowls and cloths, the smell of the food – it all spoke with affection and regret. Each girl friend had left a little of her heart in these dishes.

The cheerful students talked and ate, delighting in the bright sun, which climbed higher in the sky, generously shedding its rays on everyone. Fisheries lined the bank, one after another. Water-lilies and duckweed drifted along, twigs floated with the current, following the will of the waves. Cocoa trees shaded the camp sites on the banks. Nets, hanging from high branches, were drying in the sun.

Ever since the launch had left Grand-Bassam a group of Moslems had been studiously chewing cola nuts; others, who were more pious, sat cross-legged on their lambskins, saying their beads, reciting psalms, and singing, indifferent to the noises around them and to the conversations of their fellow passengers. The launch turned another bend in the river, and Bingerville came into view.

Houses on a hill, among the trees. Open windows, and smoke. A long, ochre-coloured building covered with old black tiles: the schoolhouse, which the 'old-timers' pointed out. The launch reduced its speed. Men, women, friends, workers, travellers, and curious bystanders were crowded together on the wharf. To the right of the wharf, canoes could be seen partially out of the water, and a little beyond them tufts of reeds, making the waves dance, swimmers, children playing, and washerwomen scrubbing their clothes. Several of them, squatting, both hands flat against their clothes, their torsos bare, their breasts of a provocative firmness, their bodies sprinkled with soap bubbles, watched the launch enter its berth alongside the wharf. Some of the women adjusted their cloths to cover their breasts, while the children played with an abandon common to children all over the world and chased each other through cascading bubbles and drops of water. The sun spangled the lagoon with brilliant flashes, reflections, and sparkles.

The launch slowed down. A man on board threw a rope to another man on the wharf, who seized it and secured it to a bollard. The luggage was taken off the launch and placed on the heads of the 'new boys' who, perspiring, began climbing the rough, rocky hill leading up to the school. A short cut through palm trees, reeds, high weeds, and giant ferns led them to the building. This path opened out on to piles of foul-smelling dung behind the latrines. A strange way for a *groupéen* to enter the *Ecole Primaire Supérieure*.

They had barely entered the school yard when a loud clamour greeted them. People ran up to them from all directions, shouting: 'New boys! New boys! The big new boys!' A great lout of a fellow planted himself in front of Climbié, who was loaded down with suitcases, and shouted right in his face: 'Well, well, what do we have here? Another new boy! It's written all over your piggish face! Come on now, what's your name? Oh, so you don't even know your name, huh?'

The newcomers heard only the words, 'New boys! New boys!' in the dormitories, the classrooms, the lavatory, everywhere. Some of the 'old-timers' would seize your ear in both hands and shout the words with all their might: 'New boy!'

And there was nothing you could do. In the dormitory the beds squeaked with the slightest movement. In the dining-hall, under a high ceiling, tables were lined up, dirty, rickety, badly jointed, coated with fly-specks, and with scraps of food in the cracks. A terraced playground; rows of Cayenne almond trees, in bloom; and carved in their bark, the names of older students from Grand-Bassam.

The most important thing now, for Climbié, was to buckle down and finish his work quickly, to be able to help his mother, for he was her only surviving child.

A European was looking out of the window. It was the Headmaster, 'Gongohi'. None of the students knew what his nickname meant. One found the word only at school, associated with the Headmaster, and graduating students had passed it on.

Gongohi was tall and fat, and his voice carried a long distance.

He always wore shoes with rubber soles, and might pop in anywhere unexpectedly. When he entered the dining-hall, the din would cease abruptly. Forks and knives no longer touched the tin bowls, even lightly, although the students usually enjoyed scraping the bottom of their dishes, just to make a noise. The Headmaster's shadow weighed so heavily over them that the boys even stopped chewing.

In the presence of the Headmaster, the bursar would distribute the students' uniforms on the first Thursday of the school year. The bursar tossed through an open window two vests, two pairs of trousers, two jackets, two towels, which one caught in mid air, disappearing immediately so as to leave room for the next student, who had to come running, stop short, catch *his* uniform on the wing, and scamper away in turn. The jacket might be too big or too small, the trousers too short or too long – this was hardly important. No bursar could stop to consider such trifles when he had a hundred boys to dress. When the night bell rang, Gongohi would make his rounds of the dormitories. The young boarders' favourite game, besides talking, was making the beds squeak. The master on duty would take down names, but the beds squeaked just the same. If he shouted, the beds squeaked even louder. If he punished everyone, the innocent could always protest. But Gongohi would arrive in silence, a flashlight in his hand. The noise stopped immediately. Stopping beside a bed at random, he would pull on the occupant's feet, and ask:

'Did you make your bed squeak?'

'No, sir.'

'Are you asleep?'

'Yes, sir.'

'Ah! He's asleep. . . . The gentleman is sleeping! Just look at this bird who sleeps with his eyes open! Are you really asleep?'

'Yes, Mr Headmaster.'

'Here! Here! The gentleman sleeps! I must be crazy then. Am I crazy?'

'No, Mr Headmaster.'

'Are you asleep?'

'No, Mr Headmaster.'

'And why aren't you asleep yet? You must be making your bed squeak then?'

'No, Mr Headmaster!'

'Well now, who is making all the beds squeak?'

During this examination all the other students, so noisy earlier, feigned sleep, their fists tightly closed. Several of them even snored. But Gongohi had only to turn his back for all the sleepers to wake up again . . . and start squeaking the beds.

A TERRIBLE INCIDENT upset life at the school. It happened during the month of June, a very rainy month.

For a week, rain had fallen without a pause, day and night. Never a clear spell, the sky uniformly grey.

On this day a soft rain was falling, unhurried, stubborn; water ran down the trees, the roofs, the terraces, the flower-beds, everywhere, carrying away sand and gravel. Sometimes a pale glimmer that vanished fast, and shortly afterwards, a low growling in the distance, very weak, like the echo of a drum. For a week the same soft, monotonous drumming had made everyone in class doze. In going backwards and forwards between the classrooms and the dormitories, without raincoats, the students ended up with all their clothes soaked. That is why, on this particular day, many students were determined not to return to class, despite the many warnings from the senior master's whistle. One of the students, Kassi, was suffering from a toothache. His left cheek was swollen.

Gongohi was standing beneath his veranda. And the late-comers had to pass in front of him. Kassi came by.

'What's wrong with you, lazy?'

'I have a toothache!'

'A toothache! Well! Take that for your toothache! Jump to it! Get to your class!'

None of the students laughed. On the contrary, a disapproving murmur ran through the class.

A little later Cissé, a 'blockhead', came by. When Gongohi raised his arm to strike him, Cissé grabbed it. Gongohi was surprised, indeed shocked. And the student said to him: 'I refuse to be beaten. I've done nothing wrong.'

They glared at each other. The rain fell. The other students held their breaths, opening their eyes very wide. Gongohi raised his other arm, and Cissé grabbed that one. The students trembled. The more cowardly ones, those who suffered everything without ever opening their mouths, kept whispering: 'That's the way to do it!' What was going to happen? This angry giant, couldn't he pulverize this runt of a student with one flick of the finger? They stood there, face to face, the student and the giant. Who would give way?

The rain went on falling with the same steadiness, the same indifference. There was a battle between men, but it was not the rain's business. Its role was only to fall, and make the rice come, the maize, the yams, the wheat, and rye, everything that needs water to grow and provides food for men and nations. The indifference of the rain became disgusting.

Finally Cissé released his grip on the Headmaster, who was shaking with anger. And that very evening, the student was expelled for 'serious misbehaviour'. He left whistling, for he knew that he had just punctured the rigid discipline of the *Groupe Scolaire Central de Bingerville*.

Gongohi wasted no time in getting on a boat. After his departure, spring came again; smiles returned to faces. Everything thawed, bloomed, flourished. The flowers seemed more beautiful, more alive with colour. In short, the young boys now breathed an atmosphere of peace and security, which made them more confident, more brotherly.

In the evening, after classes, the garden was filled with students lying on the grass, telling stories, recalling memories.

A breeze blew, carrying with it all the scents of flowers and fruits. The banana trees waved their large leaves, as if to answer the chattering parrots hurrying to get home, as if to say good-bye to the sparrows who flew by at full speed, to the swallows who chased one another in the young night. Bees gathered honey in the lemon and orange trees. They raised their heads and posed like warriors whenever the wind shook the leaves, rustled the high grasses. Then they would once again dip into the buds and flowers. In the sky little white clouds floated by: they formed layers, unravelled, and then glided into each other, forming a thousand capricious designs. And everywhere in the ambient air, the lingering fragrance of the ylang-ylangs.

The students no longer took naps. They preferred to crush the fruit of the jaca tree, which they ate after cooking it in tins. The fruit made their stomachs swell, and during the night they filled the dormitories with 'cannon shots'. The senior master, overcome by the smell, no longer took down names.

News came from the city, only to break against the wall enclosing the school, which was a world unto itself. The school had nothing in common with the lives of other men, in offices and on plantations, or so it seemed. But when the students walked to the city at night, to visit friends, they heard stories about the farmers who came in to complain against their summons for pulling down a scrub-tree or cutting a liana, a mere leaf, or for killing a monkey in a forest reserve whose limits were unmarked. It was fine to say that the service-paths were markers, but the forest obliterated the paths. . . . The farmers, constantly on the alert, took to the bush whenever they saw the cap of a *garde-cercle* in the distance. And they would come in delegations to tell the Governor that it was impossible for them to pay the taxes on newborn babies, on the dead, the disabled, the political exiles, because animals were destroying all their crops.

These tales of woe were not always taken into account. The budget would suffer, they would have side-effects of incalculable harm on the country's economy, etc.

It was after their return from one of these visits to town that the Headmaster announced a school contest to see which student would attend the Governor's banquet.

IT WAS A tradition in French West Africa for the Governors of the colonies to hold a formal banquet and ball in their palaces on 11 November and on 14 July.

In Bingerville, every profession there was represented except the farmers. The blame for it, everyone said, should fall on the Office of Political Affairs and the Criminal Investigation Department, the two arms of government held in balance by a Governor entangled in red tape and reports. No, one could not invite these bumpkins who, in between bites, would dare to say bluntly to the Governor: 'What you're doing is no good.'

At these dinners, which had become traditional, there were always the same jovial guests, sticklers for etiquette, the same priorities and exclusions.

The receptions took place with scrupulous punctilio, on the same days, at the same hours, with the same format, copied from old programmes which had been neatly filed away in locked chests. Through the routine of these receptions, like mosquitoes that carry malaria, a drowsiness in the government had spread into workshops and stores. The disease might have been insignificant in itself, except that in keeping people irritably on edge, it sharpened their suspicions of one another. Both officials and populace, suffering from the same shortsightedness, considered each other abnormal, and they all sounded each other out with nasty digs and cutting remarks.

It was in such an atmosphere of artificial friendship and peace, of latent angers and potential quarrels, that a new Governor landed, imbued with new ideas, with a head full of bold projects. He was the Prince Charming that Sleeping Beauty – the Ivory Coast – was waiting for! In a burst of activity, he would approach the farmer and say:

'Grow bananas too, my friend.'

'How will they sell?'

'The Whites will buy them from you to export.'

'They grow bananas themselves.'

'Do it anyhow.'

'And what if they don't want to buy them?'

'Do it anyhow. People will see.'

And the African farmer grew bananas, because the Governor, smiling and shaking his hand, had said he should grow bananas.

Something of a poet, loving the fresh air and the beautiful tropical sunsets, the new Governor spent long hours contemplating nature, seeking restful release from the worries of the day. It was certainly on one of his solitary walks that he noticed the school – the school with dirty yellow dormitories, finger smudges everywhere, and walls flaking off with the slightest gust of wind.

One Saturday night he went inside, accompanied by his entire general staff. It was the first time a Governor had visited the establishment. He walked through the classrooms, questioned several students, distributed gifts (one hundred sous to Climbié), and preached discipline, hard work, and courage. The Governor's itinerary did not include the cracked showers and the dining-hall with its rickety, box-like tables.

The students were fascinated with the Governor's constant smile. A Governor who smiled!

This proconsul had, nevertheless, many serious worries, profound and agonizing worries, because of the depression in business. A general crisis which hit the young colony had paralysed the treasury. It threatened by its duration to destroy the vitality, enthusiasm, and faith of the colonists. Every day the damage was worse. 'We must do something as soon as possible,' the Governor kept saying to himself. Already important firms had closed their doors, and banks their pay-windows. Not a day passed without even more startling rumours to disquiet the already crumbling spirit of the colonists even more deeply. Subsidies, aids of all kinds, special grants of money, were like cauterizing a wooden leg.

The Europeans had become extremely frugal, entangled in a budget that tightened every month; they noted the level of opened litres of aperitif, counted the lumps of sugar, weighed the open tins of preserves. And the domestic servants, also made very unhappy by all these restrictive measures, put little energy into their duties. The crisis, having reached the pocket-book, had soured dispositions.

Added to the tales of woe were recriminations, fits of anger, revolts, bankruptcies, and suicides. The colony was sliding towards an abyss. To avoid collapse, it had become necessary, at any cost, to take extreme measures – amputation or serum. The Governor chose serum.

To this end, he organized an exhibition fair where commercial men, planters, industrialists, and artists could arrange to meet one another.

This fair was indeed a success. The Governor's smile, and his alone, broke the ice which had frozen relations between these groups of men. His smile chased away the crisis, and renewed everybody's confidence.

He wanted to win over the hearts of everyone, this Governor who smiled. And perhaps that was why he had another brilliant idea: a children's festival. All the students took part in it. The fairgrounds experienced unprecedented activity. Climbié carried the flag of the *Groupe Scolaire Central*. Having assembled at the entrance to the ferry, the children went over in groups, singing, until they reached the pergola opposite the municipal buildings. They were proud to have their own festival. This day was theirs alone. They sang, danced, and ate. They felt a part of society now. They thought of themselves as a rising force.

The *gardes-cercle*, usually boorish, followed the example set by their superiors and, forcing themselves to smile, tried to pat the cheeks of the children, who fled from them, long experience having taught them that the hand of a *garde-cercle* gave a very bitter caress.

That evening, before the performance in the outdoor theatre, given by the students of the E.P.S. and those of Grand-Bassam, Climbié and Nalba walked along the noisy streets. He told her how this theatre had come to be.

With the departure of Gongohi and the arrival of B——, the school took on a new character. By improving the menu and by giving the students a certain latitude, B—— encouraged in them a liking for school life and for expressing themselves freely. The bullying also stopped.

One day, the tailor who supplied the uniforms replaced the leather buttons with gold-metal ones. The students looked like *gardes-cercle*. The occasion seemed to call for fun and games.

Akabilé, a first-year student, grabbed a baton, put his belt over his jacket and the baton through the belt, and was suddenly transformed into a sergeant of the guards, followed by two assistants. They accompanied the white man as he took the census. The Headmaster, drawn by the students' smiles, became interested in the play and its actors, and had his men weed out a large rectangular area behind the dining-hall and surround it with clusters of flowers. And there, at their leisure, the students could meet, discuss problems, or just chat. To encourage folk performances, every Saturday night was devoted to the theatre. . . .

The Governor was charmed by these magnificent performances, for they not only revealed the students' talents but were also more pertinent, more precise and complete in their statistical information than all the figures tacked on the office walls.

He now had the students on his side, along with the demanding colonists.

But he did not want to stop there, this Governor who smiled.

Having just taken stock of all that went on in the country, it was easy for him to notice the absence of a children's delegate at the traditional banquets and balls. To rectify this omission, he invited to his dinner on 11 November the best student in the *Groupe Scolaire Central* of Bingerville.

The best student in the school! This embarrassed all the teachers, for each one had his favourite student, who might not be the top scholar in the class. A contest dealing with a French subject was decided upon. Only the students of the third and fourth levels could participate. Climbié and Balo were selected as the two contestants, and almost immediately two camps were formed. To tell the truth, Balo had more people on his side than did Climbié. Both camps held meetings and played tricks on each other. Every day, more and more caricatures appeared on the blackboards, but they were quickly erased when a teacher arrived. Badges were cut out of magazines. Each camp booed the other. The Governor's banquet, you say? That was worth anything! In the dining-hall, plates flew from one table to another, and blows were exchanged for a 'yes' or a 'no'. Great louts of fellows threatened the smaller boys who, nevertheless, managed to keep calm and cool. And why not? You commit yourself, for better or worse, to a side, an idea, to a conviction! So you defend your flag, and to the devil with everything else!

The fearless Headmaster lived on the margin of this revolution which he had stirred up with his idea of a contest. The increasing number of students punished in class, in the dormitories, or sent every evening to fatigue duty, did not constitute sufficient evidence to make him think that his establishment was going badly. Every day he found a new way of exciting and keeping alive the competitiveness of the students. And with each day that passed, the fatal date of the contest loomed nearer, overheating tempers.

The meal that evening was one of the more mediocre. A storm threatened. The air was heavy, and nerves were on edge. After a heated argument in the examination hall, the two camps came to blows. Their cries and shouts were heard from far away. Ink bottles were thrown, benches were broken, and tables were overturned, unhorsing their riders.

The Headmaster, hearing the noise, ran to the room, napkin in hand, still chewing something. His students, as if in a tilting-field,

[65]

were exercising their young muscles. The Headmaster looked at them, flabbergasted. What language were they speaking? In their fury, the students had forgotten their French, as if for them it had become a dead language. The insults formed in their own dialects better punctuated the blows from their fists, and carried them faster to their goal.

The Headmaster's voice rose above the uproar, and the students remembered the French language. No one, however, wanted to tell him what had caused this brawl.

The contest took place. Balo won. His followers paraded around triumphantly. Little by little, the approaching exams turned everyone's energy back to lessons and books.

CLIMBIÉ SPENT his vacation on his uncle Assouan Koffi's plantation at Boudéa. When Climbié got off the train his uncle was waiting for him. The old man had many more wrinkles than Climbié remembered, and there were two long furrows on each side of his nose which seemed to have been carved out by sweat. Many white hairs were visible in his beard now. As the porter brought his suitcase, Climbié looked at his uncle and wondered: 'Why is he growing old so fast?' The stoop in the old man's back made him walk more slowly. 'What has happened?' Climbié kept asking himself.

Everyone they met asked the same question:

'Is that your little one?'

'Yes.'

'How nice! Little one . . . your papa is a good man. You must work hard at school, and when you grow up, you must be good like him.'

The next morning Climbié and his uncle set out on foot for the plantation, which was about forty kilometres from the city. In the small villages they saw Dioula and Haoussa pedlars sitting in front of their stalls, kettles and prayer-rugs within arm's reach. Their feet were cracked from walking, and the skin on their heads was creased from carrying goods.

As they walked on, Uncle Assouan Koffi told Climbié how he had acquired the land.

'One day, while on a trip, I saw this forest, and I decided at once to be a farmer. I must admit that, during my military service in France, one of my commanding officers called me in and said:

' "What are you going to do once your military service is over?"

' "I'm going to be a civil servant."

' "Why don't you take up farming . . . ? What you grow doesn't matter. . . ."

'I didn't take the idea seriously then, but later I decided, suddenly, to be a farmer. But, my child, that meant giving up the good life, the weddings, the dancing until dawn, and the beautiful outfits with stiffly starched collars and brand-new coats. I had decided to be a farmer. I knew the hardship of living from month to month, I knew what scrimping meant. I too have fought against expenses always greater than my income. I was always beaten, and like other people, I felt somewhere in the back of my mind the agony of tomorrow. And I also knew the struggle to hold on to the last sou, which flies away anyhow. You're wondering about my pension at retirement, but, my child, that never solves the problem. When you're old and always sick with one disease or another, and have a family to look after, how long can a small pension last, if you don't have any other income?

'Let's admit it. We took the wrong road from the start. But was this really our fault? With the coming of the Europeans, the civil-service clerk was born, all the more admirable in the eyes of people who, from then on, could not conceive that a person might finish school without becoming a clerk, whether in government or business, or, in any case, always on the side of the Europeans. We all thought like that. The European was a ruler, a very powerful lord who had his prison, who levied taxes. He made the rain fall and the sun shine. And you had to live in his wake, in his shadow, in order to have a little peace. When you saw how his messengers operated outside the cities, dressed in their black tunics and red military caps, clubs in hand, you couldn't help seeing the European as a great scourge dominating the Negro world. You placed him

D

on the same level with some evil genie of the water or bush. To serve him, to be constantly at his beck and call, was the only way to get along with him. And everyone was anxious for his child to leave school a clerk. Hence the dissatisfaction with working the land.

'To plant, to cling to the soil, to refuse to let yourself be uprooted and swept away by the torrential waves of fashion, to refuse to let yourself be tossed about in the whirlpools of more or less contradictory ideas, this, alas, was seen as the desire to remain "savage", so strong was the pull and fascination of the city.

'It's only fair to add that people fled from all the heavy taxes laid on the villages.

'You saw how well your uncle N'dabian had developed this plantation before his death. By the end of the ten months of mourning, the bush had taken over again. I had to start from scratch. You'll see! Ah, my child, there is always work to be done. Every day I struggle against the lianas, the weeds, the thorns, against the rain, wind, and sun, the insects, the marauding monkeys, the other harmful animals – and God knows there are thousands of them! I have to be on watch night and day.

'Does the wind blow too hard? Then I say to myself: "That wind will make the flowers on the coffee trees fall, and the harvest will be bad." Is the rain early? Then it's hard to burn the fields, hard to grow food-stuffs, and so there is famine. On the other hand, suppose the rain is late? Then there is still a risk of famine because the time for planting may pass. A tree falls. Did it crush my coffee? My cocoa? Your head has to work as hard as your hands. I have to see to everything myself, to be sure that it all goes well. To create a plantation is no fun, my child. And no relative will help you since you have no money. Those who do come, leave right away. They can't wait; they don't have time for that. Life goes on, you have to live, to gather in the fruits of labour quickly. But I don't rush, because I want you to continue this work that each day brings me closer to death. All my labour, all the things I've denied myself, must some day bear fruit. You must continue everything I've started. Each of us must carry a stone to the building-site.

[68]

'You are still young. . . . I will say all this many times, so that you won't forget it.

'The work! And after the work, independence, my child! To be no one's responsibility! That should be the motto of your generation. And you must always shun the man who doesn't like work.'

They had arrived. Without even stopping to rest, Uncle Assouan Koffi said to Climbié: 'Let's go watch the work.'

They started out again. Climbié did not want to leave the path because he was afraid of snakes. The vipers would nap in such heat, coiled up in the grass, and the scorpions too – they would be wandering about. But Uncle Assouan Koffi was thinking of other things. Whenever he saw a liana entwined about the foot of a cocoa or coffee tree, as if trying to strangle it, to suffocate it, he would leave the path, cut the vine with his machete, then weed out the brush from around the young plant. Before starting off again, he would stand there looking at it, not even feeling the tsetse flies on his legs, or paying any attention to the horseflies buzzing around him.

The pink leaves of the cocoa trees fluttered tranquilly. The coffee trees swayed in curls, like breaking waves. A woodpecker tapped on a tree. The weaver-birds were singing in the palm trees. Humming-birds darted from one clump of trees to another. Turtle-doves and young partridges flew up. Uncle Assouan Koffi stopped to catch his breath because he had a bad heart.

'As you see, my heart is not as strong as it used to be. But it will keep beating a while yet. We have a little farther to go before we stop. My heart may be tired, but I'm not! . . . Look at those good-for-nothing workers over there. You have to prod them with pruning shears or machetes to get any work out of them. . . . Did you notice the difference in that gust of wind just now?'

'No.'

'It's a wind that announces rain. Look over there, straight in front of you. Do you see the heavy cloud on the horizon, just above that big tree?'

'Yes.'

'Well, it never visits us without bringing rain. Listen, the touraco bird is singing too. Mark my words, it will rain tonight. Finally we'll be able to thin out the plants and replace the dead ones. . . . Those high weeds over there were all cut down just two months ago. Oh, if only my plants would grow as fast as the couch-grass and the reeds! Then I would never have to worry about what tomorrow's weather was going to be.'

They passed by the rice fields where insects, hidden in the mud, were singing. Then they came to the banana farm where taro, sugar-cane, pimento, and gumbo were also grown.

'Look there, look at that bug trying to get away,' Uncle Assouan Koffi said, pointing to some kind of beetle with black shiny wings. It was part of a battalion of insects nipping at the young shoots of maize, rice, cocoa, and coffee. 'Everything here is our enemy; they are all allied against us. But they won't have the last word. . . .'

The sun was setting. In the sky were high-piled clouds – fine soft feathers that seemed to change colours, strokes of shading, shells, ghosts, grottoes, lakes, and rolling hills, like a backdrop in the theatre. It was so good to be alive, so good to breathe the fresh air blowing by, laden with scents it had gathered here and there in its chase through the forest. How nice it would be to live there in such calmness, with the murmuring of insects and singing of birds, far away from the distracting noises of the city. Climbié was full of confidence in himself. He walked along jauntily, no longer afraid of snakes. A snail crossed his path, but he let it go since it was not the kind you could eat. The man and boy regained the main road. Swarms of colourful butterflies fluttered around puddles of water, bathed and fanned one another with their wings, anxious to hurry home. Lizards scurried through the leaves. Grasshoppers on a slope, leaning on their forelegs, stared angrily at the man and boy passing by. Ants were coming and going; some beetles pushed along an enormous load of dung. The wind rustled the grass around the coffee and cocoa plants. Some noisy toucans and parrots swooped in from far away and raced a squadron of sparrows. The swallows, on the other hand, were out for a walk. The temple-cocks kept crowing, announcing the hour of rest. The tired wind dragged itself through the grass and the ditches, stirring up the dry leaves. The uncle and the nephew walked slowly.

'Yes, my child, to be a farmer is not easy. Both man and nature are against you. Help is hard to find, and the men you do find leave again, with no reason, just when you need them the most, when it's time to sow or time to harvest. And even when you've overcome all these difficulties, you still have the very serious problem of finding a market for your products. Yet, everything considered, at least you have your independence. And that means a great deal in the life of a man, my child.'

IT WAS THE beginning of June, the time for the final school exams as well as the competitive regional ones. Already for weeks now the students had been writing letters to their parents; their desire to pass the rapidly approaching competitive exams made them nervous.

The post-office employees had no reason to love this month of June with its flood of mail. They brutally date-stamped these letters, without any respect for the ideas, the dreams, the illusions, and the courage they contained.

The students no longer knew what lessons to revise, what books to consult. During frequent question-and-answer periods, the teachers tried to fill in the gaps, for their honour was at stake. The results of the competitive exams between the eight territories of French West Africa tested the professional abilities of the teachers themselves.

Since the month of April, when the final list of candidates had been determined after three preliminary exams, school had become as busy as a beehive. Everywhere, during the evening hours, one met the candidates determined to enter Ponty – in the garden, in the classrooms, in the dormitories, on neighbouring plantations, in the streets, on trails bordering the lagoon, nestled in the high grass. The Headmaster himself, very ill-tempered on the subject of 'discipline', confessed to being satisfied with the conduct of his students.

It was in such an atmosphere of strenuous work, of dreams and apprehensions, that the exams to enter the *Ecole Normale William Ponty de Gorée* began one Monday morning, with an essay in French.

The dictation exam came on the following day, an event which prompted much discussion.

The School Inspector had decided to give the dictation himself. Unfolding the thin piece of paper, which had been placed in a sealed envelope, he read it through one, twice, reread it, and then shouted: 'Attenshun. Take your pensh in your handsh. I am going to shtart. Write!' The students lowered their heads, dipped their pens in ink, and aimed them towards their paper. The pens raced on, then hesitated and stopped, stumbled and stopped again. Several students batted their eyelids and knotted their eyebrows together, while others scratched their temples. Some passed their thumb-nails between their teeth, but most of them just raised their eyes towards the platform. They seemed to be calling all the gods to their aid. One by one the heads rose. The Inspector kept dictating. The students stared at their teachers, and their expressions seemed to cry out: 'We don't understand!' At first there was only a slight murmur, vague and imprecise, but it gradually gained form and strength, and soon filled the classroom. All that made the Inspector nervous, and he shouted even louder, to make sure everyone could hear him: 'All thoshe who, like egshaushted horsesh, balk at even a shmall obshtacle, will not inshpire shympathy from a shingle pershun.'

The erasers worked harder than the pens. And the Inspector continued to dictate, walking from one corner of the classroom to the other, his nose glued to the paper, his voice getting louder and louder.

More than one student shook his head as he saw the work of the eraser on his paper. His dreams flew away, and the *Ecole William Ponty* faded farther and farther into the distance. To fail, after so many long months of hard work, of willing refusals to go out and have fun! To fail, just because the Inspector had a provincial accent that no one was used to!

During break, the students got together and agreed to void the dictation test by refusing to take the other exams.

That afternoon the students dispersed themselves around the garden and refused to sit for the mathematics exam. Their teachers came to look for them and kept saying, without any real conviction: 'Be reasonable! You will pass. The students in the other colonies make more mistakes than you do. The Inspector speaks very well. You aren't used to his accent, that's all. . . . Come on now, let's go inside!'

Those who were strong in maths entered the classroom first, dragging their feet a little. The others were obliged to follow. But that evening, all the students in the school took off to find the Governor.

Imagine an excited, disorderly crowd of one hundred boys, their chosen delegates in the lead, climbing up the hill leading to the Governor's palace! The noise became louder and louder despite the shouts of 'Silence!' by several boys.

Looking out of their office windows, standing on their doorsteps, the Europeans and the Africans watched them go by. The boys were off to see the Governor – as if powerful men were easily seen! The Governor of their very own children's festival would surely see them! They walked on. The pebbles kicked along by their feet rolled into gutters. The birds in the mango trees, playing safe, flew away. You could go and see the Governor with a catapult in your pocket. . . .

The Governor's private secretary met them. He smiled at the boys' request to nullify the exam, and replied: 'We'll see. I will speak to the Governor.' He did speak to the Governor, but the exam was not annulled.

CLIMBIÉ HAD THE good fortune to pass. His name appeared at the bottom of the list, but none the less, among the chosen few.

There he was, on the Port-Bouet wharf, ready to board a ship, a dream that had been his for a long time. People had told him such fabulous stories about ships! When travelling on a steamer you had to be clean; if not, the motor would stop, for the motor, like a genie, does not like dirty people. When travelling on a steamer you could not eat, for you would get seasick. When travelling on a steamer. . . . What had people not told him? At last, he was going to examine one with his very own eyes.

To climb aboard a ship was already like a dream! In Grand-Bassam, Climbié had many times tried to fool the customs officers, wanting only to reach the end of the wharf where he could see the ships up close. But a sleepy officer would always open one eye and ask: 'Your papers, please?'

Retracing his steps, he would say to himself: 'One day I'll get my revenge, and I too will travel on a big steamship.' With fresh determination he would bend over his books and notebooks and immerse himself in his work. He would not even stop to chat with his friends. He flipped through his geography book, absorbed in the pictures and the maps. There was France with its provinces: Maine, Anjou, Normandie – the land of apple and pear trees which looked like young mango trees – Sologne, Limousin. . . . He looked at the names of cities: Paris, Lyon, Reims, Toulouse, Mâcon – a woman's name in the Apollonian[19] tribe – and still other names, which were written in big black letters on all the crates unloaded from cargo ships: Bordeaux, Marseille, Le Havre, Hambourg, London, Portsmouth, and New York! There were pictures of Papeete and Honolulu, with palm trees reflected in calm lakes, and young men and charming girls with flowers in their hair and unchanging smiles on their faces.

All of a sudden Climbié remembered the day a *garde-cercle* had kicked him, and his books too, because he was beating some mango trees with a pole, to make the fruit fall. Over there, with skies just as blue, countrysides just as restful, lakes just as quiet, surely people must treat one another more humanely.

He looked at the map of France again, with its multicoloured divisions, its jagged, sandy coastline. There was Paris, with its Arc de Triomphe, the Louvre, the Panthéon, the Eiffel Tower, Notre-Dame, Place de la Bastille, Place de la Nation. The last two names meant very little to Climbié. He did not see all the history in them, the continuous struggle, the slow but sure march of the French people towards the fulfilment of their destiny. For him, they were only nice-sounding names. He could not imagine all the tears, the misery, and bloodshed represented by these last two names. Place de la Bastille! Place de la Nation! The entire history of France is contained in these two names.

And always there were imaginary ships, on a vast ocean, ships very like those anchored beside the wharf. And each one carried some of Climbié's dreams – in the storerooms, in the cabins, right up the masts, clinging to the chains and ropes, in the creases of the flags. His dreams, like the wind, rushed into the sails, to give the motors more power, more energy. And the ships, throughout their voyages, in all the ports visited by Climbié in his geography book, swarmed with his dreams, binding him to all other dreamers in the world whose hearts beat in unison and who seek each other in the false dark. He was one with all those who face life with a smile. . . .

Six years had passed, and there he was, at the end of a wharf, ready to embark, all his old dreams surging through his mind, like the waves in front of him. All his returning memories seemed to spring with the waves, shatter on the beams of the wharf, then like them die away, and disperse over there on the sand glittering in the sunlight.

Each wave, like the turning of a page in a book, brought another memory to him, another image, another perfume – always something that Climbié had not thought about for a long time. He stood at the end of the wharf, bathing in the past which the ocean seemed to have preserved intact for him.

The students, surrounded by their parents and friends, argued and laughed. Climbié was alone amidst their noisy excitement, which he tried to submerge in the howl of the waves, in the squeaks of the rusty cranes, in the gutteral commands of the Kroumen[20] overseers. But in vain. Little by little the infectious excitement spread through all the happy groups of family and friends. Climbié, in order to keep his bearing, paced off the length of the wharf. How many people are there in the world who travel without anyone to wish them *'Bon Voyage'*? Is happiness ever shared? When men are deprived of their joy, don't they turn their spite against you? When a happy man is demonstratively happy, is he thinking of his sad and lonely neighbour? And Climbié felt a sharp stab every time there was a burst of laughter, for it seemed to say: 'And you, who accompanies you?'

He watched the rolling waves as they began to swell and spread out, becoming bluer and bigger as they arched higher, whitened, doubled up, then crumbling all of a sudden, went away to die in a layer of foam on the shore. He was anxious to get on the boat, to be far away from all the happy sounds. Finally, the order to embark. . . . Climbié jumped into one of the baskets. The crane lifted, then set him down in a whaleboat which a motor-launch pulled away. He could breathe now.

The *Foucauld* was in front of him, spitting water, all its engines turning. The motor-launch pulled up alongside it. The students climbed aboard while their girl friends waved good-bye from the shore. The passengers on deck watched them.

To avoid looking altogether like a 'new boy', Climbié followed behind the 'old-timers', found his bearings, and read all the instructions. Already he found himself making fun of those passengers who, wanting to go to third class, were taking the stairway to second.

At last he was on a ship! Yet he had for so long imagined what it would be like, that everything seemed dull to him.

Leaning over the rail at the stern, Climbié looked out at the countryside – fishermen, cars, the lighthouse, huts, cranes, the wharf, whaleboats, motor-launches. Through the dense foliage on the shore, he tried to see Abidjan. . . .

He had just rounded another turn in his life. *Normalien*, now *Goréen* – yes, he had grown up. Thoughts closed in on him, overlapping with one another; he could not manage to fix or analyse them. They came like whirlwinds in a storm.

Six o'clock! The *Foucauld* sounded its third and final whistle. The wharf and other boats sounded *'Bon Voyage!'* in return. A quick jerk: the engines had started up; with a supreme effort, the propellers moved the steamer, weighted down with dreams heavier than all the products taken aboard at each port. The water churned and bubbled. Always at the stern, Climbié watched as the wharf withdrew, then the trees and the countryside. A seagull followed the ship stubbornly.

Suddenly he remembered the words of Nalba: 'Don't be like the others who won't know us when they return.' And he wondered: 'What made her think I would change? How could I change?'

The seagull abandoned its course.

Sassandra! Blue sky, clear horizon, and a deep blue sea with silver reflections.

Conakry! The foothills of Fouta-Djalon[21] stood out sharply against a background of radiant sky.

Tomorrow Dakar! A farewell party was organized by the students, who danced on the deck. They were all full of attentions for the student nurses.

Sitting beside Dossou, Climbié watched the dance. Dossou was from Dahomey, and they called each other *fofo*, meaning brother. . . .

The ship glided along smoothly, in a hurry to arrive. From time to time it greeted another ship with its siren. . . .

Climbié had no desire to sleep that night; he wanted to see Dakar from a distance. He went down to his cabin where all the other boys were sleeping, rested a minute, then climbed up on deck again.

It was five o'clock when his neighbour awakened him, shouting: 'We've arrived!' With a few quick bounds, Climbié was on deck. The ship had stopped.

Lights from other ships shone everywhere. The sea was calm, calmer than a lagoon.

'What are those blue and red lights?'

'The passageway. . . . The entrance to the port. We are still on the open sea. A pilot will come to get us. It's different from Port-Bouet.'

'And what are those other lights over there?'

'Rufisque. . . .'

'It must be a beautiful town, with all those lights. . . .'

'A town like Grand-Bassam, Grand-Lahou, and Assinie. An old town with many warehouses, and old narrow-gauge tracks along its streets.'

'And Gorée?'

'Gorée is what you see over there.'

'What? . . . Is that Gorée?' replied Climbié, pointing his finger into the pre-dawn obscurity, at a sombre mass lit up by two flashing lights, in the middle of a black ocean. Nature seemed to have put it there on purpose – such a small piece of earth in such vast depths – as if to make it seem even smaller, and perhaps, by contrast, to show the true size of things to which men attach the most importance. So, was it for possession of this very small point of land, that the European states had fought one another so many long years, during their competition in Africa?

Gorée! So that was where he was going to live! What a disappointment! He had pictured Gorée all green, with tall buildings and a thousand splendours. The real Gorée looked very different.

One by one, passengers awakened and made their way to the deck, which groups of sailors were scrubbing down. One by one, lights went out. Wind rustled the women's dresses and whipped against the men's trousers. Finally day arrived, bringing with it a torrid heat and a burning thirst.

The *Foucauld* approached the harbour slowly. It passed by yellow mountain-sides where men worked and called out to one another.

'What are those?' Climbié asked one of the 'old-timers'.

'Those are mounds of peanuts. . . .'

Everywhere, people bustling about their business, continual coming and going of cars and wagons. Dakar, at least, was a city! But Gorée!

From the ship, the students transported their trunks in a launch, which dumped them on an island of tumble-down houses. Commanding all was a castle bristling with cannons. The Dahoman students unloaded sacks of flour and yams, and butts containing whole roasted pigs.

Everywhere, sand and rocks, and ancient mounts for cannon. Palm trees; cocoa trees on the northern part of the island, and a few baobabs. Young Senegalese watched the students disembark. Some were leaning from the ramparts, others against a stone wall or in a half-open door.

The next day Climbié worried his way to class. What would his new teachers be like? What kind of student would he be up against? He would have to work hard, for here they would not talk of him, but of the Ivory Coast. They would not say that 'Climbié' stands first or last in his class, but rather that 'the Ivory Coast' stands first or last. The competition would be between regions, and no longer between the students as individuals. In spite of himself, Climbié felt a weight on his shoulders. At Gorée each student upheld his own country, and wanted to impose his country on others. . . .

TO LEAVE! To be done with all these forced manners! Most of all, he hated having to say 'Monsieur' to all of his friends. That was all right for normal-school 'blockheads', but not for chaps in the same class! This over-simple conception of relationships, combined with a peaked cap which always drooped stubbornly over one eye, often earned Climbié extra fatigue duty.

After a week, each student knew his relationship to the others. Climbié no longer trembled. Mathematics, however, still refused to smile at him, and he decided once and for all not to study it.

THE HOT SEASON was severe, unbearable. The evening breeze blew in vain. A leaden atmosphere weighed over Gorée; men and beasts prayed fervently for rain. Classes were lifeless, and nerves were on edge. Palm trees, their leaves yellowing, mournfully turned their branches towards the earth. Lost clouds passed over without stopping, anxious to regroup in the thick mass over the ocean. Nevertheless, you could feel the coming of winter in the air. Sometimes, during the evening, flashes of light zigzagged across the sky. Ah! this weather which crushes, grips, suffocates, and depresses! . . .

For four days the wind had driven to the south-west the clouds banked up over the island. Yet everyone lived with the hope that the next rain was near at hand. To be able to sleep, rocked by the music of the water, was the wish of all.

Suddenly, one Friday, the sky covered over. From Rufisque, dark clouds swooped down over Gorée in heavy layers, descending almost to the level of rooftops. Several seconds of calm, and the wind broke loose. It howled, merrily upsetting everything in its way. In its fury, its rage, it swirled the sand, beat against doors and windows, and split trees. It sent leaves spinning off branches, and they flew away by the thousand. It tried to carry away the roofs, but they resisted, groaning. The traders folded their baskets, stood and waited, ready for who knows what joust. The mighty baobabs, uncertain of the outcome of their battle with the elements, merely shook their heads, while the cocoa trees and the palm trees snorted violently. Men ran. The wind hurled sand in their eyes; dogs barked and scampered off to shelter, and the first drops fell, big, thick, with a noise like hail, ricocheting off the tiles on the houses. The earth drew them in, soaked, and the water began to flow. A smell of wet sand filled the air. A wan curtain obstructed the horizon and covered the ocean. Thunder growled, off and on. Lightning gleamed palely. Everywhere, the moan of water falling that makes one dream. The curtain disappeared, and the foaming sea broke against the wooden wharf, which tried to resist it. The dormitory was flooded. A barrier of sand, bricks, stones, and brooms held out in vain. Shoes floated by, bumping against the bedframes. The students, their legs bare, splashed about in the water like children. One of the lazier boys, who had perched himself on a bed, fished for a pair of sandals. Armed with brooms, brushes, buckets, and basins, the students, singing and smoking, emptied the dormitory. Outside, the noise of the sea and thunder; inside, that of the brooms, the buckets, and the students' laughter. Standing on the first floor, one of the teachers shouted: 'Silence!' Little by little, the squall gave way to a profound calm. Men left their retreats, and windows opened. A cat, crouching in the corner of a doorway, licked its whiskers, while the storm rolled on towards Dakar.

Three years at Gorée! Three years quickly gone by! And one day, the end of school, and the beginning of vacation. It was time to leave. But there were no boats, none. For two weeks, Climbié and his friends from Dahomey, Togo, and the Ivory Coast, had dragged the weight of their nostalgia through the streets of Gorée. Tired of reading, they just walked. Whenever a launch arrived, they would run down to the promenade. From there, they would look out at the ocean, the open sea, and the launch, all of them wondering: 'When will we be able to leave?'

Close by, on the sand, waves splashed against canoes. On the wharf, a bustling crowd of servants, military men, and passengers. Over there, on a sparkling ocean, the mailboats of Casamance.[22] Farther off, Rufisque; and still farther away, Bel Air. Then the boys would run from the promenade towards the castle and settle themselves on the blocks of basalt, polished by waves which brawled about them ceaselessly. Sea urchins fought being carried out to sea by the water's ebb. A young girl opened a window, smiled and waved at the boys, stayed a moment to watch them, then pulled the curtain. The ocean growled and roared through the shredded ruins of old houses, from which, each time, it swept away a rock or plank.

Morning and night the students would scan the horizon. They were waiting for the *Brazza*.

Very often they would go to Dakar. Just loafing, they wandered through the harbour, visited the Galeries Lafayette, the Kermel market, Syrian-owned stores, bakeries, flower shops, hardware stores, and bookshops. They went everywhere. Arriving at the Sandaga market by way of Avenue William Ponty, they then turned into Avenue Maginot and climbed the hill towards the School of Medicine, where they had lunch. On the way back they would cross the Corniche, with its jagged, sharply pointed rocks, and arrive at the port in time to catch the launch to Gorée.

Every morning, Climbié and his friends would walk around the island. They would watch the military manœuvres, visit and re-visit the House of Slaves, where a peaceful family now lived. The many cells served as caves for the young tourists from Dakar. Climbié went from one cell to the other, filling them all with beings and shadows. He saw them move and pull on their chains. He heard them beg for mercy, especially the women and the young girls. Pitiless guards stood at the door. What dramas these palm trees, these cocoa trees and baobabs had seen, braving all weathers! Gorée had the appearance of an old historic town. It was no longer the little point of land that had greeted Climbié when he arrived. It was an island overflowing with history, a town where the houses talked, where the sand whispered secrets ... a town where everything told a story, related an odyssey. Men were there in the noisome obscurity of the cells. People feared their escape. Climbié would say to himself: 'Dreams began and ended here. This island and this house were relay stations, stops in a long move forward, in a voyage without a return. Men have changed people's lives as they have changed the paths of rivers. And there, where men once cried and pleaded for mercy, men today dance and sing.'

Through the door of the school, which looked out on to the ocean, Climbié would watch the waves as they came to die on the rocks. It was the door of departure, and he tried to imagine the fright which must take possession of those who pass through it to set sail and follow their destiny. He compared them to the bales of cloth, to the sacks of food, that the cargo ships loaded and un-loaded at each port. Gorée was only one depot. Sadly, he would continue his walk, wondering if anyone ever acknowledged the true worth of his fellow man.

Finally, the last night! Never was dawn awaited more impatiently. At the first crow of the cock, the students were already filling the wharf with trunks and boxes. They were happy and rowdy now, very different from those timid young boys who just yesterday had carried their sadness across the island. They jumped up and down, ran around, and waved their arms. A special launch was coming to take them to Dakar.

The *Brazza* was there, smoke pouring out of her two stacks. It was not long before she lifted anchor.

Night had come. Climbié lay in his berth, unable to sleep. His studies were over now. What next? In a few months he would be able to start work. Would he stop living with the devil in his purse? Would he ever have as much money as he needed? Would he have done better to go into medicine? Could he take three more years of school? Then, perhaps, he might have more money to help his mother.

And moreover, as a doctor, he could save human lives; as a teacher, he could help educate his people. But as a clerk? A clerk! He would spend the rest of his life filling in forms. No one would profit from what he had learned at school.

So, what did his diploma from Ponty amount to? Three years of hard work, only to arrive at a dead-end, to wind up in a garage! The way before him was plotted out. But behind him the way was no longer clear. 'The plot thickened' indeed. He had reached his second promotion, the second stage in the rise of a clerk.

Beating the water with her powerful propellers, the *Brazza* hurried along, anxious to be at Port X by H hours. She seemed to say to Climbié, who was deep in thought: '*Alea jacta est!* Do as I do. March on towards your destiny! . . .'

PART II

DESTINY called Climbié to Dakar, a city of many taverns and night clubs with such prestigious names as Oasis, Floréal, Gerbe d'Or, Lido, and Tabarin, a city of modern restaurants and cabarets, where such famous artists as Tino Rossi and Josephine Baker often performed. Adjusting to life in the capital was difficult for a newcomer, since all the problems confronted one simultaneously.

Servant boys shook the dust from rugs and bedcovers on to the heads of unfortunate pedestrians; barouche-horses made royal fun of the municipal edicts and hygiene regulations, but, on the other hand, the relations between the Europeans and Africans seemed more cordial, more human, than in the Ivory Coast, where the Europeans destroyed whatever rights to citizenship their Negro subjects had. Could one say that this friendliness was a result of the policies of the newly organized Popular Front? In everything they did, the Europeans and Africans rubbed elbows: May 1, the Government balls, etc. . . . The traffic policemen, wearing white gloves, made the African chauffeur and the European motorist obey the same laws. Climbié waited to see if the European would jump down from his car and attack the policeman, or just not bother to stop. But no, the European remained behind the wheel of his car, ready to start off again when the signal was given. The European, perhaps, did not respect the African as a man, but he respected him as a French citizen, that is, as one forced to live under the same laws.

Climbié felt perfectly safe in Dakar; people thought of him as another citizen. But then, it must be said that, in Dakar, people did not seem to make a distinction between the words 'subject' and 'citizen': both Europeans and Africans never stopped talking about Socialism, Radicalism, and Communism. The main political persuasions of the region had their 'chapels' in Dakar, their branch-offices, just like the great financial establishments. But if the latter housed themselves in large, soldily-built edifices, the former, on the contrary, took up residence in tiny, smoke-filled rooms.

Climbié read newspapers of all political tendencies, discussed politics with various leaders, and with several young colonial administrators who had been sent by the Popular Front to serve the new political structure. These young civil servants talked to Climbié about Karl Marx and Engels, Dialectic and Scientific Materialism. He listened to them. To tell the truth, he understood little of what they said. He was forced to consult a dictionary. At Ponty, none of these problems had been studied. These names had been ignored. Philosophy, sociology, civic instruction? Outside the programme. Only a higher elementary education had been given to him in preparation for his career as a civil servant. All the same, they had placed in his hands a tool, an instrument: knowledge of how to make the most of himself.

These young, enthusiastic administrators, determined to fill in all the blank spaces in all the Climbiés of this world, held meetings which, in no time at all, were declared illegal, and soon the young administrators were scattered throughout French West Africa.

But remaining behind to train Climbié was his departmental manager, a young intellectual with whom he discussed everything.

At the end of every month, he helped Climbié balance the accounts, saying to him: 'In France, it is a tradition to help the young. I'm your elder. Don't thank me. For me, it's a duty.'

Climbié had been in Dakar for six months. A compatriot invited him to the christening of one of his children. The ceremony took place in the restaurant–night club where Climbié lived. After dinner there was the customary dancing. In the courtyard, guests drank and talked. At one table the voices became louder and louder. Climbié, understanding neither Wolof nor Portuguese, only stared. The clock struck midnight.

What was happening? Two men stood up and threatened one another, grabbing each other by the necktie and the jacket collar. The fingers of one flew to the throat of the other, who struggled to free himself. The guests shouted; the women squealed and hollered. Many of the young people, who had perched on chairs, even laughed and took sides. The quarrel must have concerned something that had happened in the past, something which the drinks and music had brought to life again. Tables capsized, taking with them, in their distress, their cargo of glasses, dishes, and bottles, whose wreckage was ground under foot. The crush of people zigzagged, flowing now to one side, now to another, bellowing all the while. The screeching of women rose above everything. They gesticulated, and in their wrath knocked over bottles; some danced in pleasure at the sight of two fighting cocks, come to grips. They were waiting for the end of the battle, so that they could kiss the victor. Suddenly, a blade gleamed at the end of an arm, and no one could hold it back. The arm plunged amidst the crowd pressing around the two fighters. A cry, compounded of all the cries a human heart can hold, forced all the curious onlookers to recoil. The blood splashed upward, as if to stain the harsh white bulbs that illuminated the scene, as if to reach far above, towards the clear moon in a quiet sky. A man reeled about, faltered, stopped for a second, a minute, wanting to step forward. His feet refused, his heart refused, his whole body refused. He fell backwards, clutching himself and stamping his feet; he doubled up a moment, then stretched out and lay still. A man was dead, who only a short while ago had been eating and laughing.

There was a tragic hush. Then, gradually, the calm dissipated in a roar of people running away in panic. Someone had mentioned the police. And this one word was a reminder of the jeopardy every witness would be in. Some people scuffled at the door, hurrying to get out, to get as far away as possible from this place before the police arrived. Others grabbed their bicycles, which they held at arm's length and used as buffers in trying to force a passage; a few shouted after friends. Women called for their husbands, clutching children close to their sides.

The proprietor of the bar, a Chinese, kept shouting: 'Don't leave! Don't leave!'

'Are you crazy?' someone answered. 'Who wants to stay here? You straighten things out with the police!'

And in a twinkling, the courtyard was empty, except for the dead man, left lying there under a livid moon, his legs spread apart, in the coagulation of his own blood.

Climbié wanted to throw a *pagne* over the open eyes, but a friend restrained him, shouting: 'What do you think you're doing? Ah you – you don't know the police! You'll be the one they badger with "What happened? Why was that, now?"'

'But you can't leave a man like this, all night, with his eyes wide open?'

'Listen. One day a safe was stolen from one of the large business firms. The incident dragged on for a long time. The police had found the place where the cashbox was thrown, and plain-clothes men kept watching the spot. Everybody who passed by and saw it, was careful not to say a word. But one poor devil couldn't restrain himself from pointing it out to the police. The police questioned him for hours and hours: "Why did you walk by there? What were you planning to do? Was this the first time?" On the strength of such "whys" and "hows", the man was thrown into jail – "provisionally". That's the way of the police, my friend. You're new in Dakar. But the rest of us, we know how their justice works. You saw how fast everyone made off, didn't you?'

Having returned to his room, in the same courtyard as the bar, Climbié fastened both locks on his door, as if to stop the dead man from entering. His friend had spoken wisely.

Although Climbié was just a simple tenant, who understood neither Wolof nor Portuguese, during the next few weeks he was constantly summoned to the police station to answer 'very urgent' questions.

People now avoided him, and crossed to another pavement. Catholics crossed themselves whenever they saw him approach, and Moslems would murmur: 'Bissimilai. . . .'[23]

Several months later, the people began talking about the strike at Thiès, on the Dakar–Niger line. The railwaymen had stopped working. The military intervened, and many serious incidents occurred. The newspapers took possession of the event, and it was so often commented on, so often subject to new interpretations, that Climbié started asking himself: 'What really happened?' Not even God would know if He read all the newspapers!

The young Wolofs, thinking it wise in such circumstances to express a different point of view, started a newspaper of their own, but it was over-dynamic and lasted only a short time. It was killed by its own vitality, whose truculence scared everybody.

OVER THERE, in Europe, things were going so badly that there was general mobilization. People felt the approach of catastrophe and were powerless to stop it. And it was horrible, destructive, infernal, Dantesque. Industrialization was taking its revenge on men, and on nations. 'What would the Whites be without their guns?' the Africans kept asking themselves. 'Their civilization is so fragile, so precarious, that they have to protect and defend it. Our ancestors, at least, fought for water holes, for pasture land, for a little plot of ground, for the necessities of life, and to gain some wealth. Today one fights for Civilization, Justice, and Liberty. And the weapons are guns and bombs. To be sure, after the scuffle, one filches a little land and a great deal of money from the loser. But that is only for the sake of tradition, for if one takes up arms, it must be to defend Civilization, Justice, and Liberty, threatened by an enemy who wants to destroy the equilibrium.

'The Whites all talk about Civilization, Justice, and Liberty, and never reach an understanding. How do you expect them to understand us, we who are of another colour, and speak different languages?'

For months the recruitment offices had been besieged by enthusiastic young people eager to enlist and go off to battle.

With the black-out, Dakar took on a new character. Men in uniform roamed the streets. Every week, ships carried troops away. They could be seen arriving from the open sea one morning and disappearing the following night.

Then came the defeat of France, with its consequences, and the flourishing of the black market, lush and garish. Petty traders sold chickens in exchange for rags, so great was the shortage of cloth.

Climbié reflected on the invasion. Men, uprooted from all they had known, now walked along streets which aircraft flew over. A world excited, uncertain; a buried past, and every day, the walk towards the unknown. Fighting during the day, fighting at night. And prisoners, hostages, deportees.

The confrontation between men, will it never be anything but a brutal shock? The contact between Whites – war! The contact between Whites and Negroes – war! Always force. Snatch from the weak man his mouthful of bread, then enslave him; dance gleefully over the hecatombs and shout your victory. This is what people call the basis of Civilization, Justice, and Liberty. Those who accept this state of affairs get everything. But those who refuse servitude and ask for justice, get exile, prison, death. At dawn, whole districts are surrounded for the 'collection of taxes'. Young people are enlisted for unpaid labour in the yards, as is the custom on some African roads.

And Climbié thought about the young people in the cities, those who had deserted the difficult but peaceful existence of the village. They had surrendered the pure, healthy air of the country for the overheated, dusty air of the city. They had left the land, the warm community, the household gods – who no longer protected them against evil; they had given up everything to go to the White man's city, to lose themselves in the crowd, so that they could flee forced labour and call-up.

To read *La Moisson de 40* by Benoist-Méchin, it would appear that, up until that time, and by design, everyone had been set on making out the European to be a superman, superior to human contingencies. And that is why the edifice suddenly collapsed; the European was revealed to be only a man, just like the African, a man who could suffer, be hungry, thirsty, a man like all other men, always seeking a bit of security. Everyone had wanted to make the white man a god, to put him on a pedestal and surround him with his cinema, his frozen meats, and his bombs, forgetting that he was and will always be, before anything else, a man, and that the only dignity he had to defend was not his dignity as a European or as a White, but his dignity as a man, nothing more. For the races, by their very differences, make only a single bouquet, whose pleasant fragrance will fill the universe when every individual has found his place in the community. . . .

The stir of the agricultural shows, the attractions of different exhibitions, the great doings whenever generals or ministers arrived in the city, the village fairs and their musicians, the sporting events – these were like waves that, after they had passed, returned each individual to his own pain and worry, which they never bore away with them. Such was life in Dakar, when a crucial event happened: the attack upon the city in the month of September.

That morning, the people awakened earlier than usual. Women crowded to the public fountains to fill their basins and buckets, each one wanting to be first. The roosters put their questions to the day streaking upward. A humming-bird sang in a mango tree. A Portuguese painter, his ladder slung over his shoulder, whistled under his breath. The weather cleared visibly. In the street, a mangy dog scratched himself for fleas. One by one, the shops opened up. Housekeepers put out garbage pails on the pavements. A pair of crows had perched on an electric wire – looking like two large black knots. Swallows chased one another. A vulture hovered overhead. Dakar came alive with all its noises. Cars honked, cyclists rang their bells; the jeweller, the shoemaker, and the hairdresser were already at work. The children left for school, satchels thrown over their shoulders, and women set out to do their shopping.

Pieces of paper fluttered down from the sky, and were scattered by the wind. Men jostled one another in their hurry to catch them. A rumble of motors was heard in the distance. Nothing could be seen in the sky except tiny dots, framed by tufts of cloud. From everywhere, people began shouting: 'Aeroplanes! Aeroplanes!' They were planes dropping propaganda leaflets. The coastal batteries opened fire; a ship replied. Shells whistled over the city, heading for Médina. Houses caved in. The inhabitants, half crazy with fear, ran in all directions, everyone hurrying to get out of the city. The shops closed. Ambulances passed by at full speed; tanks too. In the harbour, the *Tacoma* was in flames. The battle had begun! Machine-guns cracked: *tac! tététété, tac!*; guns boomed. Everything shook. Aeroplanes, flying in single file, dropped their loads of explosives. There were ruins everywhere, shell holes, buildings gutted or blown apart, demolished garages, the twisted metal of cars. The sky was grey, as if a thousand factories had spit smoke for nights on end. And in the sky, gangs of kites and vultures. . . .

The day after this bombardment, there began a war of leaflets and notices posted on walls and scattered in the streets.

The newspapers always arrived with pages blanked out, and the radio would give brief news accounts, more agonizing still because of their brevity.

The news that circulated through the city was more accurate than all the messages from the Red Cross and all the radio broadcasts. No one knew exactly where the information came from. But it was there, every morning, every night. The government waged a campaign against it. But try to combat information overheard by hundreds of people and spread by thousands of mouths! . . . The invasion of 6 June brought a gleam of daylight into the dark night of uncertainty. The news circulated with lightning speed. A thousand invisible antennae transmitted it to pedestrians, cyclists, motorists: everyone snatched at it feverishly in order to pass it on. Faces hardened over the years by atrocities and moral sufferings became milder; and smiles, honest smiles this time, straight from the heart, burst forth, driving off the shadows that weighed upon hearts and spirits. Emergency loudspeakers were set up at crossroads and in public squares and halls.

Americans in their trucks whirled in and out of the city. But the carriage drivers remained unruffled and sat rigidly in their seats, not even bothering to look at them. They seemed to say: 'This is our home, this is our way.' And even the horses, as if divining the thoughts of their masters, continued on at the same trot.

The Americans brought with them cloth and food, 'swing', and chewing-gum – chewing-gum which, as soon as it was handed out, became the same as legal tender. Evidently the authorities were unaware of this encroachment on the franc and the sorry state of affairs it struggled against. Everyone was infatuated with chewing-gum, especially the women. And the hearts of the poor, at bottom, were mouldy with chewing-gum. The black market bounced back and flourished after this first landing.

Then came 8 May, and the ringing-out of the great bells in the churches, cars honking their horns, cyclists ringing their bells, sirens blowing and crowds singing, guns booming, flares crackling, ships whistling; and this news, unexpected, unbelievable, which flew through the meadows, through public squares, stations and cafés, through the stalls of Dioula traders and peanut vendors, mounting from pavement to pavement towards villas and palaces, creeping down into huts, rejoicing rich and poor; this stupendous news in which a giant, desperate war had come to an end; this unbelievable news which fell like a bomb on a city awake and waiting! People drank and broke bottles in the streets, shouting: 'Long live peace! Long live victory!' So much the worse for the many pedestrians. It was the end of the war – the end of restrictions, of miseries, and the black market, and not the least important, the end of administrative harassments.

That evening Climbié went to a friend's house. And there, with a dozen of his comrades, he celebrated the armistice. They drank more than usual. Climbié, however, had the strength to return to his room before everything started spinning around him. The bed lifted off the floor, turned upside down, came and went. The floor tiles lost their colour, they were spinning around so fast. The pieces of furniture knocked against one another. The openings, the walls zoomed in and out. Climbié grabbed the bed so as not to be thrown into the distance. The ceiling? As for the ceiling, it was making faces! Climbié did not dare get up, for fear of falling. His ears buzzed. In his head, bells were ringing, a storm whistled, and he could not stop sputtering. He smiled as he lay there, heavy-headed and alone. Ah, he, Climbié, knew what it all meant!

[93]

Nobody would find him there any more. Tomorrow the merriment would be at its peak, but he would leave the city.

Daylight came. But it was impossible to get up. Sleep was in his right leg, in his left leg, which he could not even feel; sleep coursed through his whole body, and finally reaching his eyes, settled over his lids. Which one of his ears heard the chirping of birds, and the distant din of people? Everything came to his aid in fighting sleep: children, cars, the knock-knock on neighbouring doors. Who had beaten him last night? For his whole body ached. Finally he got up. He had to leave . . . for Tiaroye.

It was impossible for him to take the first bus, because of the struggle to reach it. Another one arrived. A swarm of people rushed up to it, squeezed together like sardines; there was no room to move an arm or foot. With unbelievable slowness, it was finally loaded with lumber, huge planks, countless odds and ends. The driver talked with petty traders who walked around the coach, in the company of blind beggars. The beggars sang as they steadied themselves, one hand against the edge of the bus, the other on their canes. The apprentice driver stepped on people's fingers as he climbed down from the top where he had stacked the baggage. The driver took his seat, jiggled the hand levers. The bus refused to move. The throng of people who were standing about, began to push it. . . .

The wind surged in moaning waves through the blooming cactus and the filaos along the route. Then there was the epidemic of stops, to let someone get on or off, or for inspection by the police who, with solemn faces, counted and recounted the passengers, blackened by smoke from the gazogene.

The road was long, straight, and sticky with tar; docile pedestrians walked along the sides. Other vehicles whizzed by. The driver went slowly. Perhaps he wanted to free his passengers from the tumult of the city, from the feverish pace and the taste for an artificial life, by contact with this magnificent countryside. Everything was in motion. The banana trees with their jagged leaves rustled in the breeze; small herds of cattle disappeared down a hill, followed by a drover, his staff balanced across his shoulders. Palm trees with twisted, battered and dented trunks

[94]

offered their meagre clusters of leaves as resting places for the tired vultures.

There were also thickets of dwarf-like date trees, skeletons of baobabs, veritable spectres, and one could see bands of sparrows swoop down and attack fields of corn and millet. The ash green of cabbages blended with the dark green of tomato plants.

Sitting next to Climbié was a young Togolese named Dassí who was also going to Tiaroye, to visit friends who were *tirailleurs*.[24] Climbié looked out at the countryside and said:

'Ah, if only I knew how to paint!'

'It's not ever easy to paint things that beautiful. I've painted a little, and now I understand the look which I one day saw a sculptor throw at a customer who kept asking: "How much is this one worth?" Can you put a price in francs on privations and sleeplessness, on trances, dreams, moments of rapturous excitement or of depression and waiting? "How much is this one worth?" As if all the drama taking place inside the artist, as if everything of himself he puts into a work, could be priced! No, the worth of an artist's work is only what it awakens inside us, the flame of hope it instils, and most of all, the understanding it gives us of things. In that realm, we have work to do, to reveal our fertility, to express our culture.'

'And what if, for my part, I say that we must read a great deal, perhaps more than any other people in the world, because we are precisely at the meeting-point of two civilizations?'

'I agree! If an African doesn't read, it is because he hasn't yet acquired a liking for research and personal effort, and also, perhaps, because the chances for competition are rare.'

'It's not a question of competition, my friend, but of self-cultivation and holding your own, of being up to date; and that's why, in my opinion, we should frequent the bookshops and the libraries. We must read everything.'

'You think we don't read enough?'

'Not as much as our situation calls for – demands. We have many doors to force open. And the more we come into the open, the more the chains tighten around us. A cynic might say that the ground is cut from under us. Take the business world, for example. After having monopolized the export-import market, the large firms then branched out into retail. Now they sell biscuits by the piece, like the Anagos, syrup by the glass, like the Mossi in the market square, and bread by the slice, like the petty traders. Five years ago, that wasn't the case. To the petty African trader, it means the end, it's his eviction from the field of enterprise; for, poor fellow, he can't be an importer, much less an exporter. What chance do you give him to rise and expand when everywhere an iron pot knocks him down, abuses him?'

'The earthen pot will not have a long life. . . .'

'No, not the way things are going. All that's left for us is to knock on all the doors, like deaf people, like lunatics. . . . Somebody will be obliged eventually to come and see who is knocking. And when the door is shut in our faces, because all the jobs are taken, then we will go on looking patiently, for even in the most tightly sealed wall there is always a point where the day filters through.'

'The day. . . .'

'And we have to make the day come, by certain practical changes of our own. First: the peddling of funeral ceremonies from village to village – this ought to be abolished. Second, the left-over funds should go either to the widow or to the orphans.'[25]

'Ah, if the elders in your village could hear you!'

'And what if they did hear me? They have made up their minds to relive the past. That gives them a feeling of security, whereas we are too uncertain, really, to live for the future.

'And here is all the drama of our existence, all the instability we suffer from. Do you think the old people have kept our customs unbroken? There are subtle changes that we don't see because we haven't tried to understand. Despite everything, this attachment to the past is the strength of old people. But us – what will become of us, divided between the European and his traditions, and the old people relying on customs for their strength? A moment ago, I was talking about the absurdly long funeral ceremonies, which are in fact a business, an exploitation of people's grief, sympathy and affection. I could also mention the common drinking glass. Every child has his own drinking glass at home; he's learned the danger in using a common glass. But if, in a gathering of old people, he didn't behave like everyone else, he would expect to be pointed at.

'And these children, these babies that mothers tie on their backs when they want to dance, and who, a little later, drop off because their mothers loosened them, and a wind blew hard at just the right moment. . . . We must choose between the pleasure of dancing and the life of a child. But there's no end to similar examples.'

'The European is watching, he . . .'

'No, he sees none of all this. For him, it is all exotic, that is to say, odd, abnormal, incomprehensible. And can he make a sincere effort to understand the African? He is too busy to give himself this extra work. And I will go even further. Does he ever see the African?'

'He isn't blind, you know.'

'In the office where I work with other Africans, many Europeans walk in, look around, turn, come back, and then leave with disappointment, saying: "There is no one here." I find this hard to understand. Or, rather, I understand only too well. Another example of incomprehension. In our country, when a man arrives, no matter how great or important he is, he always makes the first greeting. A father coming home from a trip speaks first, even to his own son. A chief, returning from even a short walk, always speaks first when he sees his servants. The European, on the other hand, wants you to greet him first, even if he meets you in your home or in an office. So, if you don't rise when he walks in, he sees only furniture and says: "There is no one here." '

'There are exceptions.'

'And they confirm the rule. I have even seen some Europeans enter this same office, hat in hand, and say to an astonished apprentice: "Sir, would you be so kind as to see if Mr So-and-so is here?" '

'There now, you see?'

'New arrivals, my friend, new arrivals with their rather timid, cautious behaviour.'

'Don't be upset if the driver can't go faster. . . . I have a story of my own to tell you. It happened in Upper Togo, in the land of the Cabrese.

'One day, a missionary making his rounds said to a Cabrese patriarch who was naked: "It's sinful, all that going around naked."

'The Cabrese, without losing his temper, began a conversation. First he went "humph" three times as if to pull himself together, to tune his vocal cords, and then he asked the priest:

' "Was it not God who created the monkey?"

' "Yes."

' "Did He not make the chickens too?"

' "Yes. But why all these questions? What are you getting at?"

' "And it was still God who made the fish?"

' "Of course!"

' "Well, if God made man such as he is, He must have decided that man doesn't need fur, or feathers, or scales. Therefore, it is not a sin before God to go around naked."

'Will the European be able to understand the situation of the African, if he takes the trouble to go to the bottom of things, to stoop to the man he comes across every day?'

'To see the fuss made over certain things in our country, you wonder: "Is it because the African watches, judges, asserts his rights, that he is not always given the respect he deserves?" '

CLIMBIÉ could now exclaim: 'I've seen ten years of service!' He could display his coat of arms: an inkstand supported by intersecting pen and pencil, flanked by a ruler and an eraser, with tears in chevrons, the whole in a dirty yellow, of rancid sighs never fulfilled.

Going through the mill of ranks and stages, seasoned by long delays at the foot of each ladder, every day he numbered his dossiers scrupulously. Such was his function in the division of labour. If a number were omitted on a document, wouldn't that mean certain perdition, eternal and irreparable loss, the everlasting submersion of this piece of paper in an immense wave, muddy and putrid with all the documents borne down by streams, tributaries, creeks, rivers, and oceans of bureaucracy, from city to city, from country to country, from continent to continent? The loss of one covering document, of one identifying number for a dossier – that would mean paralysis, the end of the entire delicate machine which generations of experts have tried to perfect. Isn't it to prevent such a catastrophe that five or six copies of a document are made? And also partly as a measure of economy and prudence, as affirmed by certain official memoranda?

Climbié felt himself growing old. His budget gnawed at him constantly. One worry gave rise to another worry, and these two, coupling, engendered others. A mighty sacrifice: Climbié rejected the uniform prescribed by decree No. 510 P of 11 February, the uniform for which his predecessors had fought so many years before.

The anaemia of his pocketbook was, for Climbié, a permanent, chronic, and stubborn disease.

Nevertheless, the water which dimpled over the ramparts, hooding itself with foam, the fresh ocean-wind, small fish which fought each other for tiny dead matter at the mercy of the waves, the song of a boatman in high merriment, gulls in majestic flight with wings spread wide, dartings of white against blue; and the sun, the beautiful, kindly sun, which licked and caressed your skin – Climbié saw all these things, felt them, valued them, despite the tediums of the present and the haziness of the future.

The gentle swing of a fishing-smack on the waves, the jittering dance of another in the grip of angered elements; the frothing of the swells, their furious assaults against the sea-wall, adapting themselves to its shape, trying to defeat it, to pulverize it, the gigantic struggle of stone and angry water, the crashing of surf with its snowy crest and incoming waves, the precise and sad moment in time when you wonder which of the two will win out – Climbié saw this too, and judged it in the light of his unhealthy pocket-book. Why was his pocket-book always sick? Because the growth of business was always ahead of a Government huffing to keep up. The high cost of living was always in advance of rises in salary.

And often, in the middle of work, Climbié would lose himself in an easy but thrilling game of prognostics and calculation of probabilities. Perplexed, he would nibble at the end of his pencil and stare at the ceiling, as if to implore the gods or to call them to witness. Then he would strike the table with his fist and cry out – not like Archimedes, 'Eureka!' – but, 'All the same, that would give me five hundred francs back pay! Just think, if that works, five hundred francs!'

Then he would fold the paper and crumple it, as if to kill the distress for ever and dash his dreams of happiness.

Nor was he the only one to indulge in this game. All his fellow-workers at the office built castles in Spain too. Some of them, even before the signal to go home, had already left, as if in pursuit of all the hours that had fled, each carrying away its portion of joy and repose. They all saw themselves limping towards retirement. Hypnotized, they watched this inevitable march towards a retirement which would arrive suddenly, before they could realize any of their childhood dreams. And each one, waking from a long death-trance, would murmur to himself: 'No, no, that has to change!' The thought haunted them and overwhelmed them, at the office, in the streets, at home; it was at their heels everywhere. The harder you tried to chase it away, the more it crept inside you, encrusted itself, hidden no one knew where, leaping out unexpectedly to tell you something, then diving back as quickly.

Tired of struggling, some would get up and open the large windows. But the thought stayed with them, murmuring, and murmured so loud that, one day, on the matter of the 'zone',[26] the clerks decided to call a strike all their own.

The 'zone' is an endemic social disease, specifically colonial, which rages in bureaucratic quarters.

The 'zone' is a little like the Messiah for whom the whole world waits and waits, but a Messiah who comes, though many people do not see him, not because they are not awake, but because they are not qualified, because they have not assembled all the references which would entitle the 'zone' to stop at their house, to stir hope in their hearts and to light up their inner beings.

Look! That man who is getting out of his car, who stubs his foot and feverishly gathers up his dossiers with a grumpy air – that man is one of those who fiercely oppose standardization and extension of the 'zone'. The petty Negro clerks, on the other hand, think that it is right to extend and standardize the 'zone'.

The zone is nothing more than a cash allowance allocated to civil servants. Oh yes! Sure! at stake is that famous indemnity which two camps have never stopped fighting each other about: those for standardization and extension of the zone, and those against. Some would shout: 'It's just!' and others: 'It's a presumptuous claim!' When the letters forwarded by the labour unions continued to be ignored, the African clerks decided, well then, they would 'strike'.

T HE OCEAN, pitch-black and greasy, muttered in the holes of the sea-wall, carrying off orange skins and banana peel, match-boxes, cigarette butts, a little of everything which people had thrown out of boats and which the fish fought over. Schools of sardines enamelled the water, which muttered, crashed, and complained against the sea-wall. Europeans came and went comfortably, self-assurance on their faces and in their walk. They knew what rights the law gave them, and what privileges were bestowed on their colour and nationality.

Climbié left the wharf where boats loaded and unloaded goods amid an infernal noise of cranes and winding drums.

It was closing time for offices, stores, and workshops. The workers emerged from everywhere and hurried to Avenue Clemenceau, which led to the Labour Exchange. Most of them were dressed in second-hand clothes sent from Europe and the Americas. Would the Whites only export to Africa things that they no longer wanted?

The drums in Médina kept up a steady beat. The sounds ascended, like a prayer to the divinities, a supplication to household gods, or to the ancestors, sounds sometimes clean and distinct, like a call to assembly, sometimes howling, sepulchral, sad, winged, light and joyful. . . . And through these drums, all of Africa was speaking.

And Climbié, when he heard them, thought about all the troubled Negroes in the cities, those Negroes who were on the way to losing their laughter, their loud, hearty, thunderous, inimitable laughter, the laughter of Africa, warm and generous as the sun which breeds it, a laughter which cascades; surely you have known this laughter which, the moment it is thought to be dead, is reborn suddenly, and rings out even louder. This laughter, which is not made for the shop, or for the pavement café, and still less for an air-conditioned hotel, where it wilts and dies. This laughter of open skies and fresh air!

Many city-dwellers, gripped every day in a vice more narrow than their cares, had already bartered away their laughter for a kind of set, gloomy smile at the corner of the mouth, which dies the moment it is born, a smile without vigour, since it comes from the lips and not from the heart, which 'has to be civilized'.

The avenue leading to the Labour Exchange was black with people. On a terrace the speakers, taking turns, harangued the listeners, who punctuated every sentence with a very expressive 'Yea! Yea!' Everything about them was alive, and in vibrant communion with the speakers: heads, eyes, hands, feet. They were enraptured by the flights of oratory which came from the terraces, by the sentences which flowed in healing waves, those telling sentences, each one of which expressed what all the people assembled there were thinking, and would murmur in the street, at home, in their huts, or even at their place of work. The speakers talked of everything: meat, bread, medical aid, housing, hospitalization. . . . And they certainly spoke well!

Every passer-by stopped, and soon the wave of workers had blended with a multitude.

Climbié, standing on a small hill, studied all these men, and listened to the speakers condemn realities he had lived with, and whose burden he had supposed sometimes he alone had felt.

As if to throw fuel on the fire, to turn a red-hot iron in the gaping wound still bleeding with little accumulated grievances, pedlars went through the crowd – Peuls, Dioulas with shiny bald heads, their feet cracked and gnarled from tramping all over the country – and competing with the loud voices of the speakers, they cried up their merchandise: 'Beautiful *pagnes*! Who wants beautiful *pagnes*! *Pagnes* for the little ones! Look! *Pagnes* for the husband, for the bride! *Pagnes* to make you beautiful, to make your fiancée love you. . . . Look! The finest muslin!' They teased some of the women who chuckled as the pedlars grabbed their arms, spit long streams of saliva, lifted the hems of *boubous*, then with *pagnes* thrown over arms and shoulders, sailed after other groups of women and repeated their coaxing. Scarf pedlars arrived and joined in. Fastened on each finger they had necklaces of ivory, of every colour, bracelets, jewelled rings, and from their deep pockets they pulled out samples of perfume which they waved under your nose so that you could whiff the fragrance.

'Perfume! Good perfume! Perfume for women, perfume for men!' By then, all the peddling was making more noise than the speakers. But on that day, the men had other fish to fry. And so they did not listen.

Night came. The hour of prayer had long since passed. People never noticed, they were so absorbed in the propositions of the speakers, who were expressing in public the inner thoughts of all.

A DOG PULLED on his chain and barked. He seemed not to like the chain one bit, this dog who strained to break it. But the chain was strong, made of large links, and hooked to the wall of the house.

Clambering down a slope, on a lane overgrown with filaos, a veritable thieves' alley about which terrible stories were told of robbers, ghosts, and genies, Climbié arrived at the African quarter, a district of shanties. The Negroes at the drums forced themselves to stay awake. Some traders still remained in front of their trays. But the drums were pounding; and as long as these last drummers continued to pound, they would have the power to vanquish sleep, to overcome weariness, these Negroes who have the dancing-itch in their blood. And they would have the fortitude to get up early next morning, to be at work on time. And the drums were booming, and everybody was dancing. Any night is a festival night in Africa. Joy has no particular day, marked on a calendar. Every hour has its allotted joys, which must be plucked. After work comes dancing, relaxation. By jumping up and spinning around, you relieve yourself of the day's fatigue, which slips away with the sweat and the laughter, is put to flight by singing and the clapping of hands. You shake yourself, and the fatigue falls away, like dust falling off clothes. The drums were raging. People no longer thought about the speeches of the trade-union delegates. The time for speeches was some while ago. Now was a time for dancing, for joy.

The *griots*[27] capered about, turning round and round as they beat on their drums; and the women, urged into the circle, entered laughing, timid at first, then more and more unconstrained, carried away by the rhythm. The *griots* shouted, happy to be pleasing the people, to have them under their thumb, happy above all to prove that, despite the cinema and the gramophone, the people remained loyal to them, to those whose role was to gladden the company, to maintain tradition, to stimulate again the vitalizing fluids of the past. Their shrill voices carried until they had broken against the hard shells of houses in the European quarter, where people were even afraid to laugh out loud, because that was contrary to etiquette, contrary to good breeding. The hard shells of these respectable houses, proud to shield the Whites, reflected all the noises back to their origin. So a war was declared, of sound-waves and notes. The two hostile quarters faced each other, one of solid materials, the other of shanties. . . .

Night birds came and went in silence.

Climbié leaned his elbows on the rail of a bridge under which the water hummed. Some cats meowed as they chanced upon one another, looked to the right, then to the left, crept into enclosures, hugging the walls, ran as they crossed the street, crouched in a corner, then straightened up and left.

The drums still boomed, not far away. The wind floated the

songs over his head, then bore them off to people in the Ouakam district.

Climbié saw something in the distance, rather like smoke. Was it a low cloud from the ocean, stifling the sounds of the drums? Or was it smoke from a bonfire which somebody had fed with a fresh armful of twigs – those bonfires around which all Africa marches, in a procession of riddles, fabulous accounts, epics, tales, proverbs, and songs revived in chorus?

But a shout had come through the night. It was heard above the noise of the drums, the clapping of hands, and the howled refrains. A long, ominous shout, followed by another, by several others, by complete uproar. And the wind brought that to Climbié; it was a noise sometimes loud and near, sometimes distant, moving towards the houses with hard shells. The wind plays tricks with such human noises, scatters them about, sends them far off, sounds the alarm in its own way. For there was fire somewhere. A conflagration.

The black smoke, thick with red reflections, with streamers of flames, drew up sparks which it hurled round about.

The fire had broken out suddenly, like a purulent sore which bursts and spreads. Climbié rushed up, as did other men, and fought the fire by throwing water, sand and rocks on it. In their distraction, several people threw planks. The fire weakened for a moment. Believing it tamed, people slackened their efforts; but it blazed up again even more impulsively, fanned by the wind which suddenly had become furious, as if it had come also to struggle with the men against the fire.

The fire crackled vigorously, merrily, sometimes with a joy almost insolent, and made the rafters fall in with loud crashes. It would tolerate limitations from nobody. It destroyed the neighbouring houses too. Ah! the men had forgotten about it because it had left them in peace for a while.

The flames climbed out of a white-hot centre, rushing to outdistance the men, who were just as determined to win the battle. The fire puffed up its voice to scare them; they tightened their ranks to suffocate it. The fire spat blazing embers at them. The men threw sand and water in return. The regular firemen? The fire knew they were far away, and that if they came, it would be for the absolution. The policemen who had rushed up kept blowing whistles, but the fire crackled even louder, as if to make fun of them and say: 'Go ahead, stop me! Put me in handcuffs! . . .' Exasperated by all the bleating of whistles, it mustered all its strength and leapt to the assault of fresh rafters, other shanties. . . .

At length, the fire became sleepy and tired, above all sated. Small tongues of flame searched for new prey. You could see them rise into the air, plunge back into the hot centre, then rear up again. Some men clubbed them. The wind blew, but the flames no longer climbed. They dragged themselves along, stretched out at full length, doubled up on themselves, and died of inanition. The men kept following their tracks, although the danger had passed. . . .

The roosters announced the day, from house to house, from hut to hut, from quarter to quarter. They felt their solidarity, whether in the farmyard of a European or in that of an African. They have no illusion about their lot. So, they link 'arms' and greet one another every morning. People say the roosters are singing. No! ensnared by men, they are counting on themselves all the time.

In the streets, passers-by became more and more frequent.

Faulty taps continually coughed and hiccuped, spitting intermittently, from the depths of their insides, water tinged like blood. An alarm clock tinkled, mocking the sleep of men. Doors whined, hummed, grumbled on their hinges. The streetcar threw out a last call: *'tân ti-hin!'*

Muffled up in *pagnes*, traders went to the market-place. Pigeons cooed. The night became rosy, changing into day. Servant-boys and cooks returned to work. Stars stubbornly resisted disappearing. The Angelus tolled. Dogs barked; a locomotive wheezed; a car passed. Around the fountains, housewives bawled themselves hoarse, vying and scuffling with each other. Buckets and basins, thrown with violence, went rolling across the street to the other pavement. Windows opened, and shops. The day was there, triumphant, and it was Sunday.

Old women with prayer books in hand, and girls bouncing along on their high heels, set out towards the cathedral. . . .

With a single glance, Climbié embraced the altar, the priest, and the statue of Christ on the cross.

Usually he said his prayers with wonderful facility. He said the *Credo*, the *Pater Noster*, and the *Ave Maria*, a bit mechanically, without trying very hard to enter into the meaning of the words. He recited at a stretch, as a short time ago he had recited lessons at school. But this morning he felt embarrassed, for never before had he meditated so deeply about himself, what he was for in this world, and what other people wanted him to be like.

And he could no longer take his eyes off Christ. Much too troubled, he was unable to compose himself in prayer. He mixed up the *Credo* with the *Pater Noster*, the *Confiteor* with the *Ave Maria*. His eyes went from the men to the statues, from the statues to the priest.

Nearby Christ was flagellated, stripped of his clothes; Christ naked, robbed, crowned with thorns, beaten, hungry, thirsty. . . .

Over there, Christ had fallen under the weight of his cross, his burden, the weight of a society he had wanted better, kind to everybody, brotherly. Even for him, Climbié; and for all the other Climbiés whose beautiful dreams had never been realized.

Men seemed to be killing everything in him slowly, robbing him of his beautiful young man's dreams, draining him of the splendid trust he once had in life, even as he was nailed to it by petty necessities that callus the heart.

Oh no! He was not going to be beaten down like that. He would master the obstacles, he would keep his head high and breathe an air more pure and bracing.

The only alternative is the grave! What symbolism! What tragic reality! For there are armies of men, century after century, who march towards the grave, beaten, robbed, dispossessed, hungry. Men who cannot live; men smothered, naked, in rags, insulted at every crossroads; men always trembling and afraid. If sometimes a voice is lifted up, someone has it stifled immediately.

[107]

If an arm rises up to give a sign, it is quickly mowed down. Soon, it is a head, even more quickly cut off, a light to be extinguished because it is dazzling!

Never so much as today had Climbié understood every word of the *Pater Noster*. He looked at the priest, the bishop, the faithful. Who was it Jesus wanted to save anyhow? Was it really all men? But then, why are some men hungry, in rags, while food-stuffs are destroyed and cloth is plentiful? What is charity anyhow? Is it a capital sin to eat your fill, to live with dignity, without terror, at any time in any place? People maintain machinery but take no care of a man. They notice by the very feel of it when a typewriter is malfunctioning, but they never heed in time the haggard face of the typist.

Whose heads were those he glimpsed down there in the front row, in the dress-circle? Of course! the directors and the chiefs, who had refused to satisfy the complaints of their employees. They wanted to go on being standard-bearers, trade names, institutions. Each one was conscious of what he was, what he stood for. In short, not one of them was simply himself. They were merely well-oiled wheels, well-maintained; powerful wheels, however.

In these surroundings, they had become brothers again; but as soon as they left church they would resume their public images, their status, their livery, their strife. Here there was a truce. . . . They were soldiers of Christ, crusaders. They had sworn as much on the day of their confirmation. But all that was over. They had been young then. . . .

The priest opened his arms, closed them again, turned towards the faithful, then towards the altar, speaking aloud, murmuring prayers. Afterwards, Climbié's eyes settled again on those necks with their rolls of fat.

Ah, if only those gentlemen wanted to understand the agonizing situation of their employees! If only they wanted to understand that the social obligations of their employees were not simple!

Here, the more children you have, the more prosperous and esteemed you are. And two or three wives give you status, just as some men are given status by the number of millions they have in the bank. Brothers, cousins, relations by marriage – all are 'brothers' to the African caught between the two jaws of a vice: the European ways, which make themselves powerfully felt, and the customs already there. All things considered, Climbié preferred the warm life of a large African family, which Europeans ironically call a 'family jungle'. But these directors and chiefs understand nothing of the agonizing situation of their employees. Reasoning by analogy, they take a piece of paper, calculate the cost of rent, rice, oil, and tax, then add it up, saying: 'That's a great deal! That will be enough for them. Not one sou more, for they wouldn't know what to do with it!'

Some would marry a second or a third wife; others would throw their money away on bicycles, still others on expensive perfumes. They have no respect for money, which seems to burn their fingers, they are in such a hurry to get rid of it.

Ah, if only, some time or other, the Europeans could make a tour of the African quarter! How many things they would understand! But the African quarter is not a place to go walking in. People prefer the Corniche and the flowery beaches, open to the healthy, invigorating air which hums in the filaos and murmurs in the grasses.

Climbié kept his eyes fixed on the rolls of fat on the napes of necks. He wanted to shout what he was thinking. But he knew that people would take him for a lunatic. Even the Blacks wouldn't understand: shouting in a cathedral, in the house of God, what a scandal!

The look on Jesus' face was full of love. Love! That is the most beautiful thing in the world, but how difficult in a world where interests clash with each other, collide together and yell! Ah! if bosses would make an effort to understand their employees, if they would snap out of their apathy, and speak a human language, dependent on fewer laws, and fewer dividends, stripped clean of all ferocious, aggressive egotism; if they could unhook their eyes from statistics and diagrams – how easily things would go, because everything would revolve around brotherhood. Everything would hinge on love. But alas, self-interest speaks louder! The bosses are not like St Martin, but more like St George taming the fiery dragon and its demands. . . . And there they were, stiff, buttoned from top to toe, armoured with power and privileges, unwilling to see the slightest bit come undone.

'*Ite missa est.*' Climbié was still pensive, unable to pray. Too many thoughts jammed in his head at the same time.

The church service had ended. Climbié followed the crowd a moment, watching the young girls embrace each other; then he left for the sports arena where the striking workers were supposed to meet again.

THE ARENA WAS already black with people when he arrived. There were spectators on the benches, on the walks, on the grassy field; people sitting, standing, squatting, leaning on their elbows – an amalgam of military caps, helmets, frizzy hair, *boubous*, jackets, cast-offs, peaked caps, faded and torn berets. People kept pouring in. The delegates, standing on a covered platform, were haranguing these attentive men. Finally, the Secretary-General of the Trades Union Congress stood up, a giant with a gift for speaking: 'African comrades, we in the union have fought this battle for a long time. But today, all the workers – those of the private sector as well as those of the public sector – want to unite in a common front against exploitation.'

'Right! Go on!'

'We want, and we demand, the basic minimum for living. We want to live in real security. . . .'

'Yes!'

'As men. . . .'

The applause rose from the ground, burst from the benches, descended the steps in tight waves, frenetic, enthusiastic, then lessened, renewed its intensity, and stopped.

And the crowd of workers, ready to go on strike, poured towards the door in a wave which snatched you up brutally, as if to throw you outside.

The sky was clear blue, but to the north, a haziness at the horizon announced the coming of the Sahara winds. A rumour spread, then broke over the city: the general strike was agreed on for Monday.

Armed militia patrolled the streets. Several people risked a smile, despite the presence of guns. And the militia also smiled. Only on the sly, for their commander had the air of a man who scarcely liked to joke, who would have preferred to be playing the dandy than to be there, in the street, under the baking sun. Revolver in hand, he walked as if in a jungle. And this revolver gave him an official look, a reason to hold himself erect like that, very proper, sticking out his chest. And his eyes looked like two other guns, aimed at the people on the pavements. How a gun can give one power, can transform a man! These men were doubtlessly good men who, in any other circumstance, would not harm even a fly. But put a revolver in their hands, with ammunition in reserve, and these satanic inventions, built by man, give them another demeanour, another mentality. For them, a man is nothing more than a target, similar to the targets on shooting fields, and one must hit a bull's eye with each shot. People believe that problems can be resolved by suppressing minds or cutting off tongues. . . .

Until they have removed the causes which make heads think and mouths speak, there will be no end to removing heads and tongues, which cause other tongues and heads to be removed in turn. The representatives of repressive force will always continue to fight any inkling of understanding they may have because they consider it a weakness.

What was all Africa but a huge vat over which Europe had placed her authority, her domination, like a bronze cover? And Climbié, himself, and all the other men, and all those spectators, weren't they mere crabs fighting each other inside this vat to get a little air, a little sun? They keep climbing upon one another, only to be crushed by the bronze cover. Sometimes a hand, for reasons unknown, pokes out of this vat for a brief moment, a 'personality', and then plunges back into the darkness for reasons known only to the lords who, enthroned on high, direct the destiny of continents. . . .

Long lines of tanks and young European soldiers in field-service uniforms rejoined the 6th R.A.C. Up there, in the sky, planes were circling.

Yes, it is like that. . . . At one time or another, for either personal or political reasons, the lord lifts the cover. Immediately, all the heads emerge, arms grip the edge of the vat, men want to jump out, and like someone slapping the heads and fingers of unruly students, the lord slaps the heads and fingers of those who had believed in an ideal. And the whole world is like this, thought Climbié, as he walked towards the galleries where he had seen on display horrible pictures of extermination camps. What other causes does Europe defend besides Civilization and Justice? Order? Merely to say: 'I'm hungry, I'm cold, give me the chance to educate my children honourably, to make them good citizens' – does this interfere with order? Does order not presuppose justice? What, in fact, is the exact meaning of these words?

For ten years now, Europeans and Africans had walked along the same streets, talking about 'Bread, Peace, and Liberty'. There had been no military troops. But today, because the workers talked about striking, aeroplanes were sent to patrol the area. Would these words be for ever changing their meaning with time, latitude, and longitude?

Climbié ventured among market-women peddling their vegetables, from there headed towards the butchers who were furiously cutting up hunks of meat, arrived at the fish stall where it was difficult to breathe, then turned back, brushing everywhere against the rumps of women – great rumps, emaciated and flat rumps, plump and dancing rumps, shouting rumps, and deaf rumps, rumps which spoke and rumps which kept themselves silently modest. There were rumps which made *pagnes* and dresses wave, and others which came and went without motion, as if intimidated by the noises around them. And all these women carried heavy shopping-bags whose overflow kept belching out with every step.

Climbié made his way towards the port.

How cool it was beneath the filaos, alive with mating crows!

In the town-hall garden, men were playing bowls; women sat on benches, knitting, legs crossed, their prams near them. From time to time, they would lean over their babies, then sit up again, smiling. Like the black woman whose husband goes on strike, the European woman only wants her children to be well cared for, everything about them to glow with health, and no cloud ever to come to dull their eyes. Every woman would like to see her children live happily, and for as long as possible. Do not all mothers, the world over, think in the same way? Are not all hearts made of flesh, and capable of suffering, of understanding? Why suffocate these feelings out of selfishness? or out of vanity?

Children chased each other through alley-ways covered with sea-shells.

From the closed stores came smells of naphtha, perfume, and tar, of leather, tobacco, and dry fish.

The flaming sun gnawed at the shadows which it had driven back under the trees, thrust its blades towards their dense rows, gutting them, scattered them under the thin rose trees, fought with the tufts of liana vines, under the huge baobabs armoured with leaves.

He was enjoying himself too, this naughty sun, caressing the ebony busts of a group of washerwomen who sang and played more than they washed. He would not listen to reason, this voluptuous sun, until they had, all of them, finally showed him their breasts. Then he would rest on them, lovingly, feel them, glisten on their black breasts like headlights, lift them, nibble them, then, swooning, pale with sensual pleasure, he would sparkle with all his might.

THE STRIKE HAD lasted a week. Famine had come to many households. Wives, in order to let their husbands hold out to the end, pawned their jewellery. Then one day when the newspapers were screaming about the political strike, the Colonial Minister decided to tour this corner of his territory. . . .

Drums covered with dust came out of their hiding-places. They kept coming: the Moorish drums, the drums of Casamance, which could be mistaken for drums from the southern part of the Ivory Coast.

One by one, the men and women made up their minds to play. They flung themselves on their drums, and from everywhere other women and other children rushed up, making the motley crowd larger on the pavements of Avenues Clemenceau and Liberty, which the cortège was to follow. The singers, having rolled up the sleeves of their *boubous*, flailed their arms in the air with all their might in time with the rhythm of the drums, which had gone crazy. The sun shone on all the black faces where sweat had pearled itself like tears. The crowd sang with gusto, deliriously, for it was awaiting the Colonial Minister who must be 'received with the pomp befitting a person of his rank', this Minister who was certainly going to solve the problems caused by the strike. But the illustrious visitor was late. They would wait for him! Twenty hours! Finally he was there, passing in front of them. A long line of cars filed by, amid a frenzy of hurrahs, singing, and applause.

He had been gone for a long time, the Colonial Minister, but the drums in the African quarter sounded even more brilliant, summoning everyone to rejoice. . . .

THE MONSTER BELLOWED, huffed, whistled, vomited smoke, spat live charcoal, belched ashes. All around it, calls, shouts, tears, squeals mixed together, thickened, and climbed, crowned by the blasts of the station-master's whistle and the 'whoosh-whoosh' of the engine as it jerked to a start, carrying away its cargo of men and women, its share of laughter and anxiety, dreams and wretchedness, silence and noise.

This gigantic centipede danced on the rails, to the rhythm of its own music. It took a corner, whistling even louder, as if to make fun of Climbié, who had just missed it. In the sky, swirls of sparks, and in their path, drifting ashes. At the railroad crossing the bar lowered, and the cars, one by one, came to a halt.

Climbié watched it leave, thoroughly annoyed. He had to be at Saint-Louis that very day. It was an order. He was expected that evening, and here he was at the Dakar station, suitcase in hand.

He was angry at all the people dressed in long *boubous* who, at the entrance to the station, had prevented his running fast enough. Every time he was making headway he was caught immediately in the *boubou* of some man or some woman. One solid *boubou* blocked the gateway. And nobody was ever in a hurry to move, content to prolong the good-byes and hold a friend by the hand.

'What am I going to do?' Climbié wondered as he left the station.

'Hey there, Climbié, what's happened?'

'I missed the train.'

'Get up too late? Seven o'clock, it's seven o'clock, my friend. With the train, it's like in the army,' said M. Targe, a European photographer.

'Oh, it's quite a story, M. Targe. With my requisition, I was only entitled to fourth-class. For two days, I took steps to travel second-class, at my own expense. First, after depositing my provision card at Sandaga, I went to the travel office for another requisition. I had to wait my turn. When my turn came round, the person who had to sign the paper wasn't there. An hour of waiting. Having got my requisition, I hurried to the station. The station-master insisted that the authorization of transfer be at the bottom of the requisition.'

'And again. . . .'

'I returned to the travel office.'

'Which was closed. . . .'

'You've guessed it. And this morning I was trying to explain this to the station-master, when he suddenly left to signal the train to be off.'

'What are you going to do?'

'I don't really know. . . .'

'Climb aboard that delivery-van. In two hours at the latest I must be off myself for Saint-Louis. Before that, we'll have breakfast, then get a tankful of gas in the car, do a little checking-up on vital parts, and then, hop! we're off. I'll take you by the

Metropole to pick up a snack. We'll have a picnic on the way. I'll be with congenial friends. There's no standing on ceremony with them. Good men, very good, I should say.'

'Newcomers to the country?'

'No, no! People who have been here for years and years. And why do you ask that? So, are you all convinced that the old colonists are only loud mouths? Even among the new arrivals you talk about, there are some queer fish. It's a question of character.'

'And the influence of the climate?'

'That's bunk. We have moments of crisis. That happens to anybody. It happens to us in Europe, as it happens to you too, here. There are moments of blues, because, well. . . . A man has his bad times. And he cries. But that passes. As for me, I've been in the colonies fifteen years, and just as I wouldn't tolerate some things in France, I don't tolerate them here, either. When a man leaves a place, he takes his character with him. I have African friends; I call them by their first names because, for me, that's friendlier. I make no distinction between them and my European friends. You know that. . . .'

'How many of you in Dakar are like that, though?'

'Quite a number.'

'We could wish that you might be more numerous, more numerous than the kind who hold us at arm's length, so to speak, and threaten us with a whipping. For you well know that there are actions and attitudes which speak louder than words. And when we are up against Whites, we analyse everything . . . like big, watchful children. . . .'

'We are all men, forced to live together. You have a proverb here which says: "The goat grazes where it is fastened." As for us, we are fastened here by our interests. There are differences in character, in education. We are trying to normalize relations by giving you our manners. That will take time. For the moment, what must our attitude be? We must be patient. You must try to understand us, and we must try to know you, so that we can have harmony, even peace in our coming together. We must learn to speak the same language.'

'It's often the opposite, alas!'

[116]

'What?'

'Oh yes, when a Frenchman says to you "go", it means "you must leave". But when an Ewé says "go" to you, he means "come".'

'That's straight out of the Tower of Babel! And even more reason why we have to get to know each other. . . . Our role is to say: I am not White; I am not African. After all, are we not all men with the same rights?'

'I'm happy to hear you say this, but what about the others? How many Europeans do you think there are in all of Dakar, for example, who have contacts with the Africans? I'm not talking about daily contact with an employee or a servant boy, but only about the other type of contact where you argue problems.'

'I must admit there are few. We discuss matters among ourselves, and you, among yourselves. And that furthers nothing.'

'But we watch the Europeans, we study them. We know their manners. Who at least tries to make some effort to destroy the barriers? We do, because that person opposite us is afraid of being submerged. . . . That's why he builds barriers, barbed wire entanglements, why he barricades himself in his house, in his own quarter, after working hours. I even wonder if he shuts his windows at night when our impertinent drums come to disturb his calculations and reveries.'

'Come on now! Come on!'

'Oh yes, the quarters seem to stare at each other like wild beasts; and the social classes make me think of the class levels in a school. People can climb higher only if they pass an exam. And no matter how capable you may be, you still remain the first in the fourth or third level. . . .

'Since we've been standing here talking, we seem to be an anachronism. Africans look at us; Europeans look at us . . . No one seems to understand. . . .'

'These Europeans are like Diderot's Persians! But they have good reason to look at us . . . at you especially, you Africans.'

'Ah!'

'Oh yes, my friend! Think now. You entered our history preceded by a strong reputation. People thought you could cure the

King of France of a certain illness. Today, it is we who cure you. . . . And the European wonders where all your therapeutical knowledge has gone to. . . . Then, there is your skin colour: a result of the sun on the pigments. Look at my arms, they are burned. Well, the Europeans must be afraid that one day they will all wake up as Negroes. Come on now, an end to all this chatter! It's time to go. We risk spending the whole day here arguing. We have many interests that merge, overlap, cross, and collide. We mustn't forget that it's the same for the entire human community. One must hope that an osmosis occurs between us, by deeds and not by words.

'The motto of a Republic is a dream that mankind is marching towards. This is how the motto must be understood, for your own peace of mind and the pursuit of your efforts to find a better climate. Régimes are also weights which men hold up. When they fall, there are always victims, on one side or the other. . . . I know what I'm saying. In your country, there are men who aren't good. There are men in our country who are fundamentally bad. It's their nature. Let's guard against generalizing and, without ever giving up, let's patiently keep looking for the ways to come together, so that we can shake hands, as I now give my hand to you. . . . Yes, let us shake hands as friends; and, following the example of Pasteur, let us not ask a person what his political opinions are, or his religious beliefs, but what is the sum of his sufferings. . . .'

ONE HAD TO see the reverence with which the grasses bowed to speed! They lowered their heads to the right and to the left, swept the soil with their tops, whispered, shivered, happy to have paid their court to the new god who, in his passage, sows fire and death. . . .

The delivery van tore along. Palm trees dotted the landscape, like pins on a military map. The wind howled in Climbié's ears. The van bounced, bucked, dipped, slowed with a shudder, devoured the distance. The road stretching straight ahead inhaled the vehicle. Pebbles hit the mudguards: 'Zing, clack! zing, clack!' Scrub trees and baobabs fought for possession of the land. In the distance, the landscape looked like a tousled head of hair, crimped and tufted. . . .

Climbié would have liked to see ash-green, flaky trunks caparisoned by liana vines, with cornices of leaves and powerful branches, trees thrusting up in a crazily vigorous race towards the sun; but he saw only scrub trees and baobabs, deformed, gouty, one-armed, baobabs eaten with scurf. He wanted to see real trees, and he saw only skeletons. He looked around for authentic undergrowth, but as far as his sight extended, there was veritable desert, a savannah wrinkled with paths. He wanted to hear a chorus of birds singing the joy of living together, to see them flitting and skipping from branch to branch, as if to greet you! Ah, where are you— birds of jet, birds of fire, emerald birds, birds of azure, bards of the forests, and jewels of the water and sky, of the Ivory Coast! Where are you all, to have left the field open to swallows and crows who parade their vulgar plumage?

Thorn trees, thorny scrub everywhere; cashews, mangoes, and some mimosa. In the villages, chickens scattered, men cried out in greeting, sheep bounded over ditches and frisked over the savannah, dogs chased the van, barking.

Date trees gave way to filaos again, the grasses to baobabs, the baobabs to palm trees, and the palm trees to bushes. Farther on, the palm trees bunched together, formed a curtain, ran a while, became less and less frequent, then trailed off. . . .

A hill, corkscrew turns, and suddenly the heat gave way to a great blast of chill air. The smell of marshland, of peat. Mangroves, pelicans, lush green grass, moss, turf. A river! A real river! The water hollowed and bumped, crinkled, rippled, waved; squadrons of birds flew over, while a motorboat flaking through it made the water look old.

Saint-Louis!

'Here you are in Saint-Louis, well ahead of the train you missed this morning. Is this your first time in the town?'

'Yes.'

'There are the administrative offices, the Post Office, the

General Council, the church, the high school, the public square, under the vigilant eye of General Faidherbe.[28] Let's pay no attention to the wailing of the toads. Let's look instead at the flowers, which are truly beautiful. The garrison office, the Governor's Palace.'

'And why is that black cover over the light, on top of the palace?'

'I thought you would ask that. Well now, I'll tell you. In Florian's fable, the monkey forgot "to light his lantern", and Governments always like doing that too – or rather, very wisely, they hide their light under a bushel, under the cover we see up there.'

'God forbid, in Saint-Louis, at least, that the Government's actions be any less florid than its terraces of roses, all blooming under the joyous sun, its zinnias, tulips, dahlias, amaranths, its everlasting flowers.'

'Amen,' replied M. Targe, who was still laughing when he left. . . .

Saint-Louis was an old town which, like all others of its type, made up for its lack of beauty by its hospitality. A constant smile on the lips of the people, who all seemed to know each other, veiled the scurf and stippled wounds, the nicks, wrinkles, and mange of the walls. Many-storied houses, balconies, gateways for carriages, open sewers. Signs blinded the one eye of streets. A denuded palm tree, which one mistook for a giant aspergillum waved by an invisible hand, as if blessing men; drivers on their wobbly, whining carts; women in thick muslin, servants lugging heavy sacks of food. In front of shoemakers' shops and jewellery stores, the old people, their heads wrapped in turbans, read newspapers, and following the lines with their fingers, commented on the day's events. Pedlars, cigarette butts behind their ears, walked by, holding wide-eyed chickens by the legs. In front of a door, a furnace crackled and threw sparks in all directions.

Across the way, staked out by cocoa trees, the river, so calm, so still, looked like denuded land, scraped and levelled. Not the slightest breeze. A bakery. Look at that shouting, gesticulating line of people, that long ribbon of women, men, and children, out of which hands rise suddenly, like the tentacles of an octopus, to grab a lintel, a shoulder, a *pagne*, a *boubou*, a jacket!

Cats on doorsteps watched you go by. . . .

Why was that mob on the wharf, and why the congestion of barges, tugs, and sailing boats? The departure of a convoy up-river. A veritable market-place had been set up there. People were selling bread, mangoes, dates, guavas, jujubes, lemons of all sizes, peanuts, sandals, perfume, etc. . . . Wolofs, Peuls, Moors, soldiers, women, policemen – everyone came and went, slipping over bales of cloth, elbowing each other, talking, bursting into laughter, calling out to each other. Women intentionally threw out their hips and smiled. Men, as if by mistake, rubbed against them lewdly. Dock-hands were loading a steamship. Lying on a slab of zinc, a sentry, fully equipped, stirred sleepily, his head hidden under a canvas cover. The water shone like a mirror. A young fellow made advances to a girl who, leaning against a wall at a street corner, stared at her feet, which were dyed with henna.

The engine whirred. Standing on the gangway, a European, his hands in the pockets of his khaki shorts, was getting some fresh air, his blue shirt filling with wind. A Moroccan contractor repeated the final instructions to his agent. Three short blasts of the siren. A swirl of water. The cables slowly emerged from the waves, strained, grated against the sides of the barges, whined, and tautened. A violent shake, and the convoy got under way. Three more short blasts of the whistle, which the passengers tried to muffle by clapping and shouting. Handkerchiefs and arms lifted to wave good-bye.

The *Boufflers* and the *Sabran*, inseparable steamships, once again started up the river, beginning their bi-monthly journey, continuing their old romance.

Climbié had been at Saint-Louis in Senegal for two months. He was now on his way to Sor, on the road leading to Dagana. The landscape was lovely, and the sky was blue, pure blue, with here and there white dots, wisps of cloud. The wind was blowing, soft, cool, tender, brisk, caressing the shrubs and the mangroves,

[121]

crisping the lakes and the marshlands which were tinted with rust, clay, and slime. A steady smell of rotten grass went to his head like perfume and reminded him of his own country. . . .

A man passed by, playing on a flute. The water made pretty smilets on the banks where shellfish were crawling about. In the distance, very far away, were cocoa trees, like tiny bouquets of flowers. Vultures glided over. Rams passed by, their silken beards in ugly twists, and left behind them that unmistakable smell which distinguishes their tribe from other domestic animals. A cow, tired of waiting, lowed and called for the herdsman, but he was whispering sweet nothings to a pretty Peul girl sitting, lissome as a serpent, under a flamboyant tree in full bloom.

You seemed to be able to touch the wind, this tender, caressing wind which moved over the body with a sound like a crumpling *pagne*; this dizzying wind, which one wanted to breathe in and breathe in for ever, this wind that glided through your fingers and crooned softly in your ears.

As he watched the swells of ocean, as he breathed in the smell of marshland, and, during the evening, fished in the lakes, as he saw young swimmers frolic in the water near by, nostalgia came over Climbié, more and more each day. The river on one side, the ocean on the other. Just like Grand-Bassam! Time to leave. He felt himself a stranger now. He realized that the people here spoke another language. At home, the hibiscus was redder. The water at home had another song; at home, the wind, even more tender, gathered fragrances and brought them a longer distance. . . . He no longer felt anything or saw anything without comparing it to what he had known at home, in his own country, which now he dreamed of night and day.

CLIMBIÉ TOOK a deep breath of the air whipping against his face and tickling his ears. Along the streets, the trees were rustling. He stared at the houses as if to etch their lines in his mind, slowed down at one point to absorb his impressions, sat somewhere, he didn't know why exactly, perhaps to carry away with him a last memory of this city. His joy was radiant, infectious. In his pocket were his discharge papers, right there in his pocket, after two long months of waiting. And yet, he could have wished not to leave. Dakar held him back, enchained him, by memories which kept reviving day after day. And only a few boats stopped at Port-Bouet. Time to leave! He ran to the Harbour-master's office, and from there pushed his way forward to the docks, which were congested with cargo, motor-boats, and merchandise. Seamen bawled out from the decks of boats, while other people, landsmen, fussed about noisily, stowing, loading, and hauling. Everywhere, sacks of salt, lines of Renaults, piles of boxes. Around the tar barrels, a sticky, black, gleaming pool. And dock attendants kept watch over this waste. No one considered plugging the barrels or setting them upright. Here and there, chassis springs, car tyres, sewer pipes, cases of onions, aperitifs, liqueurs, tobacco, barrels of wine, piles of buckets and pans; rows of jeeps, boards, rails, iron rods, and so on and so on. . . . Two customs officers sitting on a box, side by side, verified papers, while a guard in baggy pantaloons, atop a mountain of canvas-covered merchandise, searched himself for fleas. Three workers near an old carriage were eating peanuts; and the ocean all along the pier was black with fuel oil. Pigeons flew out from between the stacks of manufactured products.

A hairless dog, lying on an old piece of packing cloth, crunched an old bone.

Departure, in the tropics, is an enormously tiresome business. You have to enter here, exit there, knock at this door, join that queue, wait your turn, come back, run to the Navigation Agency, to the Maritime Transports office, to the Harbour-master's office, the Passenger Bureau; and everywhere you wait for hours, in order to get the slightest information. Time? Huh! In the tropics it means nothing, ever. . . .

The steamer *Agen* was laid up. Early in the morning, Climbié ran over to USIMA.[29]

'No, we can't take any passengers.'

'Not even on deck?'

'No, sir.'

He ran to the office of Smith and Krafft.

'Is the *Marie-Paul* taking passengers?'

'We don't know yet. That depends on the Captain and on the Maritime Transport Service.'

Climbié went to the latter office.

'Excuse me, sir. Does the *Marie-Paul* stop at Port-Bouet?'

'Yes.'

'Does she take passengers?'

'Certainly. But that's the business of the Smith and Krafft office, not ours.'

'They sent me to you.'

'I just don't understand it. Every time it's this way. Hold on, here comes the ship's captain.'

'Good morning, Captain.'

'Good morning, my friend.'

'Please, are you taking passengers for Port-Bouet?'

'Port-Bouet, Port-Bouet. I don't know what port I'm supposed to hit. They never tell us until the last moment, till the hour we leave. Talk about a muddle! After all, we aren't at war any more, you know. Passengers? Hmph! All in all, I guess not.'

'Not even one deck passenger?'

'Are you alone?'

'Yes.'

'Do you have much luggage?'

'Two boxes of about fifty kilos each. And one suitcase.'

'Oh well, all right. We'll see. Come back again.'

'When do you leave?'

'Not for ten days. Actually, we've had a breakdown.'

The only thing left for Climbié to do was to approach the Director of the Harbour-master's office and introduce himself to this man's cousin, the second-in-command on the *Marie-Paul*. . . .

At last, Climbié was going! The *Marie-Paul* had lifted anchor. On the wharf, friends waved their handkerchiefs. As he got farther away, the ties which held him to Dakar broke, one by one, despite himself. Memories seethed in Climbié; faces passed before him and came back; voices and laughter rang softly in his ears. No, he wanted to get off! This town was under his skin. But the boat kept moving on. Little by little the visions blurred, the laughter and the murmuring became confused with the noise of machines, with the brewing of water under the propellers, the howling of the wind in the rigging.

The water tower, the spire on the Palace of Justice, the dome and the two bells of the cathedral, the Pasteur Institute, villas hidden in the greenery, Cap Manuel and its green sweep fringed with white foam; then Gorée, the hospital, the mosque, the castle . . . and farther on, tufts of filaos at Bel-Air; sailing-boats returning to port. In the distance, the 'Mamelles'.[30] The propellers growled, lifting and lowering the boat. On the ocean, oil slicks; and always the water boiling towards the surface.

A sailor saw Climbié standing on deck to write, called him over and gave him a table; his name was Diaw. The mate, M. Geline, to whom Climbié had been recommended by the cousin in the Harbour-master's office, came down to install a light between decks.

'You are comfortable, are you?'

'Comfortable enough.'

'Your mattress is all right?'

'Yes.'

'Have you eaten?'

'Yes.'

'Who with? I gave orders to the head waiter to give you a full meal.'

'He did, and I ate after the sailors.'

'You can eat with them if you make a friend or two. And besides, you shouldn't stay alone; walk around, talk with the crew.'

Climbié was quartered in the storage area, among joists, tools, ladders, empty barrels, boxes, and so on. There was just enough room for his camp-bed. Above him, the machines, making thunderous noises, shook the cargo.

When he got up, seagulls were flying over the ship. All the sailors, White or Negro, were bare-foot, washing the deck in teams. At last, away from Dakar . . . away from the dances, the cinema, away from the beautiful midnight suppers. Ah, those Christmases! the procession of beacons with a *griot* in the lead, followed by gaily dressed women clapping their hands, and children carrying lampions. As for him, he had invited his friends. They ate, drank, and danced; and then, towards dawn, everyone walked down the streets, rejoicing, singing all the time, waking up other friends. Guitar and banjo accompanied them. And some singing solo, others in chorus, would repeat: *'Ehoulé yo! djatchi min man m'ni min laïf tchi.'*[31]

The seductive rhythm would call other people out of their houses, who swelled the number of singers. These were the things he could do no longer, because, in the Ivory Coast, people did not know about them.

And Diaw told humorous stories, stories of this sort:

'A man had signed a pact with Death, saying to her: "I don't refuse to die, since I have to die anyhow."

' "You're a wise man."

' "But I ask you only one thing."

' "I'm not difficult, you know that."

' "Don't ever kill me suddenly. You have to warn me."

' "Don't give it a thought."

'Many years passed, and then one day Death came up to him and said: "It's time. Come with me."

' "Excuse me, but what about our pact? You didn't give me warning."

' "What? Didn't I warn you?"

' "Absolutely not! And the proof is that I'm not ready to leave this way."

' "I didn't warn you? What about that day you had a headache? And the day you had a stomach ache? And what about the time you had dysentery?"

' "That is no way to warn a person."

' "Well now, that's the way I warn everybody else, day after day. Come, we must leave."

'The man left, with Death. But on the way, under a tree laden with ripe fruit, and near a beautiful cool spring, they found three young men who had come together there, three lazy young men driven out by their fathers.

'The first had a terrible hunger. Lying on his back, his mouth open, he looked up at the pieces of ripe fruit, within arm's reach. But he didn't have the courage to raise his hand, to pluck them and eat.

'The second had a piece of fruit near his lips. He was so lazy, he couldn't open his mouth and bite it.

'The third man was thirsty. Really thirsty! Lying near the spring, water in his hands, he couldn't muster up strength to bring the water to his mouth.

'The man and Death looked at them a moment. Then, before going on their way, the man said to Death:

' "Death, tell me, which of those young men is the laziest?"

'Death walked on, pondering the question. Suddenly she turned around, and no one was there. The man had run away. Enraged, out of control, Death began searching for him. And she has been searching ever since. And when in her wanderings she sees anyone even slightly resembling the man who tricked her, she grabs him suddenly, saying: "You've been warned already."

'The man protests vehemently, but Death is like the Monitor Lizard who says: "Before I was deaf, I heard. And what I have in my head is what I heard before I became deaf."

'And many people, when it comes to this important problem of hearing, are like the great lizard. They can no longer make the slightest effort to adapt themselves, to understand new facts, to put themselves on a footing with new generations. They are deaf, fossilized in their attitudes, crystallized in their principles. They have become statues . . . the statues of an epoch. . . .'

Climbié began day-dreaming.

'Look, there's Elisa! She had been angry because he chose not to dance with her one evening. It wasn't his fault, beaux kept churning around her so. Some stayed there all the time and never went back to their places. She signalled to him. But that kind of battle was not much to his liking. To run over and quarrel for milady! . . .

'Don't pass by so quickly, Jeannie! . . . Do you remember the flowers you sent him on his birthday? It was only the second time he had ever received flowers on such an occasion. . . . And your card? You left, and you never came back. Because he didn't ask you to come back? Wait a minute, one word more!

'His first telephone call. How he shouted into the contraption! The others looked at him smilingly. He knew now how ridiculous he had looked; because he had heard people talking loud on the telephone, he had thought that to make himself heard at the other end of the line, he must always talk loud. . . .'

The freighter made headway laboriously. And the farther away it got, the more sharply detailed were Climbié's memories, in an unbroken chain. He saw people swarming in the streets, in the markets, entering stores, coming out of them again; women shuffling along, calabashes in hand, on the way to Sandaga. . . .

'Oh yes you did, Jeanie! You promised to come back. Don't go away. Why such a face? Smile, so your beautiful dimples will deepen and your eyes shine. . . . Come on now, Jeanie, smile. . . . A little more distinctly. . . . Smile. . . .'

But Jeanie melted into grey sky, low and sunless, over a languid ocean. Drops of rain. No more of those beautiful foamings and light blues in the water when it is stirred, ploughed into large mounds by the powerful propellers.

Engine failure.

At the noon meal, because Climbié was a second-class passenger and had agreed to travel steerage, the steward offered him neither bread nor wine; and the cook, who served three courses, offered him only one, saying to him:

'You don't work; you don't have any right to eat.'

'But I'm a passenger.'

'We don't carry passengers, only cargo, and we work on this ship. Even the Captain helps out.'

'Do you treat all your passengers like this?'

'You – you're steerage, and that's our business. The Captain looks after the others. Begging won't get you anywhere.'

'Don't let's make an issue of it, gentlemen. Look, all the sailors over there have given me some of each course they were served.'

'Too bad for them. You get nothing from us. You're just a use-less mouth to feed.'

'What's going on here?' interrupted the boatswain Marca Diarisso. 'Let this man alone. He's as much a passenger as the others. Just because he's steerage it doesn't mean he isn't one of your passengers. . . .'

'Then let him find a cabin, and f— off. For the moment, he's steerage . . . and what's more, he's a useless mouth to feed. You're a worker, bos'n, but him? He just piddles around!'

'Have you been at sea a long time, bos'n?'

'Since 1928. But I first started with the air-mail service. I knew Mermoz[32] when he was just beginning. I and my mates often repaired his planes for him.'

The lines thrown by the sailors tightened suddenly. The boat-swain dashed over, pulled and pulled. The Europeans ran over, and they pulled too. Three tunny were jolted on to the deck.

'The roughest trip is from Dakar to Natal, because of the whirlpools. There have been seafarers who, even after ten years of experience, have quit when they reached Natal.'

Another line strained. Everyone dashed over. Even the Captain, who was enjoying himself alongside the sailors. A colonial on board, M. B——, standing on the gangway, his hands in his pockets, watched the scene at a distance from above. But the laughter became so rollicking that he came closer. He was not the same style of man as the Captain. Climbié saw that a new class of Europeans was rising, a class of colonials, half-European, half-African, with a special idiom which would make itself felt in time. When in Africa, these men would always think of their home town. And once returned to their own country, they would hurry to get back to Africa, because, at home, their attitudes were out of place, and often hurt people's feelings. They muster in vain in the hotels, in their quarters; to protect and justify themselves they keep building structures of reinforced concrete. But Africa catches up with them, claws them, marks them for ever. They have the blues in Africa. They have nostalgia in Europe. They are no longer men of one continent, but a hybrid species. And that is a role which most of them joke about – until the truth dawns on them that they are subject to the terrible, inhuman law of 'the struggle for survival'.

The European is sometimes slow to realize the mark of Africa on him. The generous life, the wide-open spaces captivate him, overcome him, mould him, despite himself. One day he lets slip a word, an expression, adopts an attitude, and he realizes a change in himself. He tries to struggle, to keep the old standards intact. ... Very quickly he is defeated, and the wave carries him off. ... If he should try to struggle a long time, he would risk making himself oddly conspicuous. ...

And this same phenomenon is noticeable in the new breed of young Africans who are out of tune with their own environment. ...

M. B—— walked back and forth, talking with the Captain.

'What are you thinking about, bos'n?'

'I have a lot of things on my mind. We need money, much money, to become civilized. Money is civilization. So long as we don't have money, so long as we aren't rich, we'll be nothing in the eyes of the Whites. Money is essential to them.'

'You think that without money, we'll never be. ...'

'What can you do without money? But the white man calculates before giving us money. For if he gave us a great deal, do you think that I, Diarisso, would keep on knocking about the world? I would settle down in business for myself and attend to my own affairs. Who then would come to my house and tell me what to do? There are people who talk about courage, faith. ... Money confers all that. If you have money, everyone prays for you, and people acknowledge all your good qualities. ...'

The boatswain lit a cigarette, sighed, stared at the horizon where streaks of lightning flashed in intervals, crossed his legs, and continued:

'With money, we could carry on coast-to-coast trade, for example.'

[130]

'You think so?'

'Oh, yes! Who could stop me from doing it, if I had my own money? I was in Europe for thirteen years, and I've travelled a bit everywhere. I know how a man can shift for himself. . . .'

'The Europeans stick together when it comes to money matters, you very well know that. They demand one guarantee from their fellow citizens, but they would demand four from you, because you would be very warmly recommended, and from me, twenty. . . .'

'One could kill this European racism. All it would need would be for men of good will to shake the Europeans' hand, openly, and form a powerful assembly around him, a warm assembly, so warm, so brotherly, that it suffocates him! I mean it! Here's a story to illustrate it. It happened in Conakry. A native sergeant landed with a European woman. A truly beautiful woman. When she passed by, everyone stopped to look at her. Some Europeans, out of jealousy, managed to have her husband put in prison. My God! Ah, but you should have heard the woman speak at the hearing. She said:

' "Gentlemen! It might appear strange to you that we marry Negroes. For us, there is nothing unusual about it. During the war, in our country, they helped us to live in a time when one continually wondered what the next day would be like. We had neither servant-boys nor food to throw around. It is open to you to practice racism. In France, we know the word because it is in the dictionary. It is not in our actions, in our deeds, or in our thoughts. It does not exist. I therefore ask you to release my husband." '

'Ah, they were glowing that day, those judges in Conakry. They came to their senses! My God!'

'No wonder,' protested Diaw, a sailor, trying to go one better. 'That was in Conakry. Once I was in port and went into a store to buy a pair of shoes. The salesman refused to sell them, because the owner had ordered him not to sell anything to the Africans. I said nothing. That afternoon I went back.

' "Hey, salesman, give me two pairs of shoes."

' "We don't sell them."

' "Why are they on display then?"

' "That's no concern of yours." '

'So I took out my knife, jabbed it into the counter, and shouted: "Give me two pairs of shoes!" My three friends, who liked brawls, did the same.

' "Hey, Mamadou," the owner called out, "who are these natives?"

' "Sir, they are Senegalese, French citizens."

' "But gentlemen, you must show your papers. You understand, we don't want to feed the black market." '

'You see, my friend,' interrupted the boatswain, 'the Whites are like that. We have to protest, protest, and keep protesting. The white man knows you are right. But he wants you to protest, to talk, to write. He wants to give everything without seeming to. And that makes for more papers, and a lot of palaver. Everybody resists . . . one because he can't wait any longer, the other because he doesn't want to be upset all the time. And then it ends with nobody's knowing any more who is right. Every office becomes a tomb for papers. And these poor papers are a Lazarus without friends like Jesus to resurrect them. Ah! My God! Yes, obviously, an important person has one of them dug up sometimes, but the others rest in their sarcophagi, up on shelves.'

'All the same, offices aren't oubliettes, bos'n. . . .'

'I'm only telling you what people say. Me, I'm just a sailor. . . . But when I have to have my papers stamped. . . . Hmph! my friend, it's the same old story of "Go over there" and "Come back". . . .'

The rosy sun went down. A gull flew after the boat. The ocean was the colour of bromide.

Marca Diarisso, the boatswain, lit another cigarette, which he smoked as he chewed cola, and, always talkative, went on with his stories.

'My friend, the Whites trick us. They say one thing and do something else. They say, go to the right, while they, at the same time, are going left. They say, for example, that the stories of the Karamokos[33] are false, but they themselves often go to fortune-tellers and astrologers. I know what I'm talking about!'

'Hold on,' replied Diaw. 'Someone told me that before building the floating bridge at Abidjan the engineer should have begged forgiveness from the genies of the Ebrié people, who didn't want this bridge. Result, the bridge sank. And among the victims, not a single European, not a single Ebrié, because they knew the bridge was going to sink. For the Vridi canal, the same difficulties: the section of the canal dug during the day filled in again during the night. Men died like flies, because the spirits of the place didn't want the canal. It had to be dug elsewhere.'

'People say that, once upon a time, a hunter had gone into the bush. He was on his way out when he saw a pregnant chimpanzee. He aimed his gun. The chimpanzee showed the hunter her belly, and tried to ask his mercy by making signs. The man didn't want to hear anything. He pulled the trigger and killed the animal. When he arrived home, he found his wife dead. She was pregnant too. How do you explain that, my friends?

'In Dakar, there are even ghost taxis, ghost passengers, and a big barrel which rolls down certain streets every night.'

'Come on now, bos'n! . . . Rolling barrels?'

'So, you think I make up fantasies? What I'm saying is true. Ask all the old Wolofs . . . they'll confirm the facts . . . and they will tell you still more wonders! Ah! you don't know our country. . . . The Whites are beginning to understand it better than you, because you don't want to believe in anything any more. You always insist upon proof. You think that one can go around giving proofs for everything in life? Lips are shut with fear lest the mouth tell all. Life, for us, is a voyage, which is best made with joyful companions. And that's why our drums sing out the joy of farming side by side, of harvesting together, of building our houses the same way. Life, why it's a beautiful song which ought to be sung together, hands clapping all the time. It's the warm community of little and great, weak and strong, young and old, all helping one another and linking arms against hostile forces.

'Everyone felt like somebody important in the society. And that gave him confidence in himself.

'Things are taking a different turn now. Everyone dances by trampling on others. The man with a gun slams the butt-end down on the man who doesn't yet have a gun. . . .

'No! my friends, is it living never to sing together or dance together?'

Sassandra! The ocean was yellow for several kilometres. A small lighthouse, the residency, the dispensary. A stump of wharf from which whaleboats pulled away, one, two, four, bearing Kroumen[34] workers. They came with their work-kits, wearing straw hats on their heads and clad in sweaters. Several were almost naked. They took the boat by assault, climbed over the rigging, scurried about everywhere. Among them, children.

Before an attentive audience, an old Krouman told stories of his adventures. He had been more or less all over the southern seas. Their chief strutted about with dignity, like a cockatoo. He measured off his steps, premeditated his movements.

The *Marie-Paul* lifted anchor. The coast was a wall of trees with a white edge. A bay here and there, a small hollowed-out valley which cut into the curtain like a hair parting. And sometimes, a short-lived fringe of white, like lacework: the waves frilly with foam.

Evening. Night. Men slept on the decks, rolled up in covers. Climbié was on the look-out for the red lighthouse of Port-Bouet. Inside him a drama was enacting itself, a struggle of past with present. He went to bed but scarcely slept, as when one apprehends a danger, or is haunted by a question. After four hours he ran to the deck. The lighthouse. At last, he was home. . . . Little by little, other feelings came over him. . . . The veil of fog unravelled, dissipated, and the festoon of trees reappeared, deep green, one might even say black. The screen of trees had notched openings, crowns of flowers. Behind it rose small plateaux with fan-shaped ferns and corymbs whose black bases were bluish in places. The wharf was getting closer. A flotilla of fishermen. In the distance, small shacks covered with red tiles, and near by, buoys playing at porpoises. The waves hurrying shorewards whitened at the foot of the wharf. Five ships waiting to dock. And everywhere, silence. For there was a strike.

Departure is not everything. You must get back to shore, and there was Climbié, stuck . . . in the harbour at Port-Bouet, some two hundred metres from a wharf whose cranes were silent. And on the road from Abidjan to Bassam, an intense traffic, overflowing activity. Outwardly, nothing seemed to have changed; the boom, the wharf, the government buildings, the colours were the same as on the day he went aboard ship. But in like measure, the spirit of the place had taken an extraordinary turn. A strike! Did people at home know about such things? During the construction of the Port-Bouet wharf, some of the European workers had gone on strike. They had been sent home as a matter of course. Today, the strikers were Africans, friends, asserting their rights, getting angry, and leaving him to count the waves. There was chaos, darkness in Climbié's mind. Leaning over the rail, eating scarcely at all, he stared at the moving cars. Everybody saw him and smiled.

'Do you think – do you think the men will get satisfaction?' a European stoker asked him.

'Why not?'

'You're very naïve then. The rest of us know the story here. Do you see, over there, the two ships marked XF? Well, they're boats of the first slave-traders from Bordeaux. They were the first to transport Negroes. They were the first to make them suffer. It must also be admitted that Europe in those days was not very sure that it was dealing with human beings when it came to Negroes. Today, millionaires multiply factories all over France, fill them up with workers, and send you old, worn-out freighters which will carry off all the riches of this country. You know nothing of all that, you people here. In France, at Bordeaux, Marseille, Nantes, these men are known. Fingers are pointed at them. But they have money, and consequently, a voice, whereas those of us who sweat and strain as hard as those Negroes on strike, we can wait.'

'I came here in 1940,' said a greaser, 'to pick up two thousand *tirailleurs*, just as if I were after lumber for European sawmills or manpower for canneries on the islands. My God! Will men never see the difference in value between one thing and another?'

A young Algerian interrupted:

'I wish we could land. But here we are, left treading water. If only there were a port. . . .'

The greaser started up.

'A port! It's under construction.'

'And has been for how long, my friend?'

'For how long, you ask? Ports, railroads, and all that – did you have them in Algeria before we got there? Now you have them! It takes money to build all that.'

'Come on! We know that old tune. Take your old record off, and play me something else, something new. In Algeria, we . . .'

'You? What did you have in Algeria before the French got there?'

One of the four lines suddenly tightened as if to snap. Everyone threw themselves on it. Climbié was relieved; the turn of the conversation had made him a little uneasy. . . .

A log drifted by, swung to the left, swung to the right. At night the ventilators groaned in their iron cages. And all around the lights, the flying ants lost their wings.

Another night without sleep, more choppy than the one before.

In the morning, slack water, so sluggish that it looked like an immense mirror. Grease and oil splotched over it in caricatures, frescoes, animals, gulfs, phantoms, lines, a thousand arabesques. The strike was continuing. The Captain decided to put Climbié ashore. At 10 o'clock a dinghy was put down on the water, and it took him to the foot of the wharf, along with the deck-boy,[35] M. Géline the mate, and the boatswain. Climbié climbed up the rope-ladder.

At last, here he was on the wharf. . . . Home. Why had he got off? It was so hot. He had felt better out there, on board ship. Why had he left Dakar, where he had found a place for himself and had taken up its habits? He had become a stranger to his own country. Twelve years of absence! He would have to start life over again, and be involved in difficulties that he had overcome in Dakar. . . . Who would know him any more in this country? The proof: no cars or taxis wanted to stop and pick him up. Oh, if only he could get back on the *Marie-Paul*. But then what? The ship was still there, beckoning him to come. . . . Was he not at his destination? Out there was the Captain, descending to the deck; the greaser was out there, the Algerian, the Breton machinist, the baker.

Below the wharf, the boom waved brokenly, knocking against the piles covered with seaweed and shells.

Women loaded down with heavy baskets of yams were returning from the fields under a sweltering sun, their bodies dripping with sweat. They chatted, smiled, argued.

Nobody there when he left. Nobody there when he came back. Always alone. Worse yet, as though everything rejected him, no car wanted to stop and take him to Abidjan.

Dakar, its streets, its traffic, his friends passed before his eyes, and voices whispered in his ears:

'We told you not to leave, and he who goes home is not always happy. . . . You see for yourself. You are more than a stranger, you wave at people who no longer recognize you. There are others along the way who answer you . . . out of courtesy. You had to climb up a rope to get on the wharf. . . . You forced your way into the city. . . .'

Finally a small truck stopped, and all the whisperings ceased. Climbié rolled towards Abidjan. A girl-cousin who recognized him had given him two mangoes. Climbié stared at them. These two mangoes which he held in his hands were mangoes from his own country! nourished by the soil of his country! watered by the rains, swayed by the winds, and ripened by the sun of his country! A sun different from all 'the other suns'! And this wind blowing, making the heat go away, this wind had the same freshness as all the other winds. . . . And the trees, the *azobé* trees with rose-coloured leaves . . . real trees, and the birds. How could he have stayed away so long, away from these trees, these birds, the wind, the sun?

Wide-eyed, Climbié looked to the right and to the left, breathing through his nose and mouth at the same time. He wanted to immerse himself in the wind, to bathe in it, to be all new . . . to become once again a child twelve years old. . . .

The first night, a night disturbed by the gasping of the power station. A night full of noises. Sometimes Climbié thought he was still on the boat whose engines he heard idling, and ventilators whirring. His bed pitched. When he awakened, rain, a soft rain by way of greeting, bidding him welcome.

Climbié got up very early, wanting to be present at the awakening of creatures and things.

The streets were dark. In front of some houses, a small island of light, and other lights which leaked through the chinks in hovels. A cough, whispers, a creaky bed, a sigh, a door whining. Cats, seated on their hind paws, were staring straight ahead. Cars on the floating bridge jingled over the iron plates of the joints. A traveller balancing a trunk on his head made his way towards the station. Over there, a stirring of shadows. The muezzins sang. Seated in the mosque, the faithful were already praying. The market-place slowly filled with people and the usual noises. The air brightened. Birds in the trees, chirping, fluttering about. An apprentice put water in his truck. . . . The stores opened, people went to their work. Cyclists argued the right-of-way with taxi drivers and with the pedestrians on the pavements. . . . Climbié was finally home. . . . Everywhere women in *pagnes*, men in *pagnes* . . . the dress of Southern people. . . . He wanted to put himself on a level with the gamut of creatures and things. . . . For he remembered still the words of Nalba: 'Don't be like the others who won't know us when they return.'

The soccer match between Grand-Bassam and Bouaké, the South against the North, was a big event. In the Géo-André stadium, the Europeans who came from the North rooted for Bouaké, while those from the South sided with Grand-Bassam. And all the spectators, in the stands and on the green, clapped their hands, shouted, stamped about, more energetic than the players themselves. How they kicked, butted, and elbowed each other.

The ball whistled, roared, squealed under the kicks of the players hurrying wildly to score goals. All breathing stopped. All eyes followed the ball in its trajectory, urging it on or anxiously holding it back. Some people, with their elbows, helped the ball to fly faster; some clapped their hands to encourage it, others to frighten it.

Some spectators in the stands gripped the ball between their legs until it arrived at the goal. The referee, the poor referee, was liked by nobody, for he had become Fate: he held in his whistle the doom of either team. The ball was put in play again.

'That's it! faster ... faster ... aw....'

'Good!'

'Oh! poor devil, and so close to the goal!'

'You saw it, he couldn't score....'

'That team from Bassam is sharp. They'll win the cup.'

'Why you – you're blind! And what about that nice play of Bouaké!...'

The ball, scared and tired, wanted to rest a minute, and over the fence it went.... 'At last!' Ah, you think so, do you! You don't see the spectator at your heels. He paid, and he intends to be satisfied. So, the ball took its place again, under hundreds of pairs of eyes annoyed by its running away.

Europeans and Africans, in a sporting mood, tapped one another on the shoulder and spoke familiarly:

'You see, my friend, we're beating Bouaké.'

'Nonsense.... We'll beat you.'

All distance between them was abolished. And Climbié, standing near an orange-vendor, who was expertly peeling her fruit, looked at the people in the stands, the people on the green, at all those men whom joy had overcome and united, and he said to himself: 'Ah, if this harmony, this open cordiality could last!...'

The 'Alternate' 121 was the first train in the Ivory Coast after the strike. It came down from Bobo with infernal noise, driving away silence all along its route and in the stations. Crowds packed to watch it. Whoosh! Whoosh! Its noise rose above all the noises of the city and of all its quarters. It arrived in a spray of smoke and a whirlwind of cinders from igniting firewood, crammed in its boiler all along the way. Whoosh! Whoosh! The locomotive seemed happy to be back on its run....

But still, no products were brought to market. Cocoa, coffee, cola nuts – the farmers refused to sell them unless prices were raised. There were ringleaders; they had to be hunted out. In front of the shops, no activity. When a truck of goods arrived, not even the Syrians would budge. And the Africans became busily active, demanding. . . .

Climbié was considered an agitator. That is, anti-French. The tricolour ensign, perched high over the Governor's Residence, enveloped the French nationals, their characters and their habits, with its majestic shadow. And whoever dared defy the least of them, whoever dared to protest at any iniquity whatsoever, was accused of being revolutionary and considered an enemy of France; for every Frenchman, individually, saw himself as representing France.

Climbié and his friends, because of their speeches and their newspaper articles, had, people said, stirred up the peaceful farmers, who now refused to sell their products. Even the women no longer brought in the leaves which were used to wrap cola nuts. That had never happened before. And worse still, these natives had the gall to demand the dismissal of their French-appointed chiefs and came in groups to press the *Commandants de Cercle* into taking action. Such behaviour was unacceptable, because it was liable to 'disturb public order'.

The Commandant of Agbomoua gave orders that Climbié was not to be admitted to the offices of the *Cercle*. He went anyhow, under a thousand pretexts. One day the Commandant's deputy tried to order him off the veranda where he was chatting with a garage-keeper whom he knew. There was very nearly a brawl. But he continued to talk and continued to write.

Climbié came to be seen as unassimilable, indigestible. He was the *bête noire* of the Commandant who, in his reports, accused him of spreading disorder and urged his arrest. If for nothing else, as an example to others. Bad seed – dig it out and throw it away, destroy it; just like the others, the clerks who, for the same reasons, were spending their time in disruption – stamp it out; just like those other men who refused to surrender at the Caudine Forks.

[140]

As soon as people are set on ruining respectable men, vile fellows are hoisted up on deck and heaped with honours and privileges.

Really now, one didn't expect trouble from the likes of Climbié and his friends.

He had not been given schooling to become an obstructionist. Having broken the contract, having betrayed the confidence placed in him, he had become a traitor, a rebel, and, in a case like that, one could stretch the law, for the simple reason that he had wilfully put himself outside it.

So, when there was a general round-up, they capitalized on it and arrested him.

Behind Climbié the door was pulled back violently, as if to bar the light from penetrating his cell, to make him realize how good it had been to be able to come and go freely, as he pleased. For him the leaves would dance on their stalks no longer, the reflections of light would play on the trees no longer. He was now a man without rights, the property of the Commissioner of Police, the examining judge, and the bailiff; a man nobody could see without presenting first a special paper, a permission to associate. Between him and other men, the 'clean' men, there was a wall bristling with broken bottles, the yellow wall which made one's eyes hurt.

High above, a patch of sky, across which the sun moved. It ignored the struggling of men. It shone on all alike. . . .

In the sickly shadow of the cells, a group of prisoners talked and made plans. The walls were scribbled over with graffiti and messages, but, most of all, with numerous lines stroked in charcoal. By this means, men counted the days, the months, the years, at the end of which they could step through the great gateway and its squad of watching attendants.

Climbié was now in the same prison that used to catch his eye when, not so long ago, he went to the big garden. The flag still steered with the wind. His curiosity was more than satisfied. So, this is how prison was: a large courtyard, rooms in common, a few openings near the wall, bars, double doors. The signal every evening to go to bed, and in the morning, the coop thrown open. And every Saturday, visits by relatives, comforting visits which

[141]

made you forget the choking heat of the place, the fleas, the atmosphere of tension.

And the trips to the hospital too!

Climbié stared at the countryside as if he had never seen it before. He took deep breaths and held in the air before letting it go suddenly. He was storing up air, as if there were none at all in the prison. He stared at the river water, that water which he had bathed in so many times; he stared at it as if he could imprison its colour, its fluidity, in his eyes. He was anxious to capture all these sights so that he could parade them again, one by one, in his cell. He would have wished, as he walked, never to reach an end; what he wanted was a long journey, a very long journey, so that, taking his time, he could breathe fresh, healthy air, gaze at the grass, the palm trees, the reeds, the mango trees, come across free men, without policemen behind them, men who could stop if they wanted to and leave again if it seemed good to them. And birds, singing, fluttering, hopping about.

Often, at night, he reviewed the accusations brought against him. The word *anti-French*, though never put in writing, kept cropping up in every sentence. He had been sent here, to think it over, between these walls where he would feel himself a creature at the mercy of the Judge, the Attorney, the *Commandant de Cercle*, the Military Police, the Commissioner of Police, the Bailiff, the Guards – all those watchful guardians who stood for Law, Order, and Society. They had been able to order him out during a night of pick-ups, and . . . Was he not a creature on the loose, a snake it was good to stamp out? And who has ever been blamed for killing a snake? Quite the opposite! You are congratulated and all that. If he went to the hospital, even the doctor treated him rudely, and wouldn't touch him. Was he all that dangerous? He had tried to think for himself, to make judgements. All the trouble had started right there. He had wanted to play another role in society than the obscure one of a second-class citizen imperfectly trained, badly paid, and because of this, always involved in the worst difficulties. He had wanted to sing to people of the splendour of life, which some individuals strive their utmost to make ugly. Between four walls, in the dark. But nobody could stop him from thinking what he thought, from believing that every man has a right to a minimum of respect, a minimum of welfare, a minimum of liberty and security, without which he could never be fulfilled. . . . Now as soon as one mentions welfare some men become alarmed; if one mentions contentment, they think of less production, because the worker would no longer be spurred on by need, by anxiety . . . for their sake, he has to be kept tied down.

And they all tremble as soon as one mentions a little freedom. Many of them see an immediate end to all authority. The misunderstanding is right there.

Is it that certain words, on the lips of an African, have a different meaning? Climbié did not want to think about it. But can anybody stop thinking?

He, Climbié, was an 'object', because he was not a natural-born French citizen. He did not even have the same value, juridically, as all the naturalized friends who were there with him. What did he have a right to? To a straw mat – and, when funds permitted – to an old mess-tin, rusty and dirty, to a stinking meal cooked in a gasoline drum, to a bed-time of 5 p.m. No right to a bed, to covers, to meals brought from a hotel, to any of the advantages associated with the rank of French citizen.

Yes, it was here in prison that the inequalities showed up most boldly. And his friends had renounced all their advantages in order to lead the same life as he did. Every Frenchman, individually, wants to represent the Nation. And he, what was he supposed to represent? What place in the harmonious order, really, did anybody want to give him?

A prisoner involved in a number of criminal activities had escaped, so as to avoid talking or giving names. Everyone in the prison knew about his powerful connections. The day after this escape, it was they, Climbié and the others, whom the judge came to investigate, even ripping apart the linings of their shorts, in search of heaven knows what document, examining the wall and the ground to uncover a hiding place.

No, they never look for the real causes. But always for instigators, scapegoats!

This twenty-year-old judge, in the name of Law, undressed him, Climbié, who was nearing forty. And if he had protested or refused, this would have been 'contempt of court'. Everywhere, nothing but pitfalls. Is a prisoner still a man in the eyes of police power? For this judge behaved in identical fashion towards Climbié's friends who were naturalized citizens. Clearly, he was determined to make them understand that, unlike them, he was French by birth and not by decree . . . and, consequently, they also could be treated as 'objects' by a young man twenty years old, armed with the Law.

The first night after their arrival, an outraged policeman had shouted: 'Put all these bandits in a cell for me, and don't anybody let them out before ten o'clock tomorrow.'

Bandits! That was the tip-off, the notion underlying the black-list.

There are people who gamble and know how, and others who, playing with deep emotion, do not know how. This policeman and this judge fall into the second category. Despite the centuries of culture on which they can plume themselves, they remain headstrong men obsessed with one idea . . . 'aimed' men, so to speak.

Since the end of the war, some Europeans, their attitudes changed because they realize that their interests are tied to those of the natives, and that an era is completely over, have made visible efforts to smooth away difficulties and establish bridges between people. But are they heard? Political and economic necessity speaks louder. And they become, therefore, a little like con-scientious objectors in a milieu where one is always researching 'the African', as Diogenes looked for a man, studying him as one would study a rock or a plant, forgetting that he is a man also, of a different colour to be sure, but a man just the same. Is it a good reason to deal with him this way just because he did not invent the wheel? And how many of the Europeans who have such cavalier attitudes about his predicament would have been able to invent the wheel? What have they personally invented? Intelli-gence and genius are not the prerogative of any one continent, race, or colour. But the white man, outside his continent, wants to reduce everything to himself, subordinate everything to his colour. Instinctively, one could say. By right of conquest? Spirit of solidarity? Calculation? France and France overseas! That's where the answer lies, in the 'overseas'. This determinative is somewhat restricting.

Some talk too much about the barbarous past. A people is rather likely to be misjudged if the only ones called to testify are their conquerors or individuals who were forced, in the circumstances, to take up arms.

As for Climbié, he was ignorant, and he knew it; his diploma was no good. But the 'genuine diplomas' were going to come, and what place would their owners have? A little room would be made for some of them, the first; and the others? They would wander at random, looking for a position.

What does the White man want? Stability; contentment; comfort; everyday security for himself and his loved ones. The *status quo*. For one must be man enough to admit that it is very hard to part with rights and prerogatives, merely for humanitarian reasons. So, what attitude do you take towards the dependents of yesterday who, after hauling themselves up to your height, want to surpass you? It is 'normal' to strike at them, to strike them on the head, as old men strike children who want the same pillow that they have.[36] And one strikes down the Climbiés and their associates whom life has not yet matured enough.

Beings different from oneself! Several young Europeans, classmates of Climbié, who were school drop-outs, are today important people. It is hardly a matter of the stars. For the Africans who left school also, at the same time, live where they can and do not know where to turn. They become worn out in the beaten paths. During a moment of rugged going when it was all they could do to hold on, they reached out eagerly and came tumbling down. Is the race after fortune, then, over a slippery carpet which the black man is not accustomed to?

Climbié knew people in this country who, if they had been Europeans, would have occupied very important positions because of their ancient family and social rank. But they are who they are, and live as they have to. And even the young presume to bully them, because they are who they are. Ah, how nice it is to be the child of a great, strong, and powerful nation! How comforting, to look over a map and whisper with pride: 'All that is for me, the earth, the people, the sky!' That is where some of the unfortunate attitudes originate.

In response to a remark made by one of the counsels for the defence, the examining judge had replied: 'The prison is not a palace. We aren't going to give beds to people who never had them in their own homes!'

He was just beginning his career; Climbié and his friends, every one of them, had at least fifteen years of service. But they must stay at the bottom of the ladder. Their sphere.

The moon, through the bars, brightened the room. In the neighbouring cells, men were snoring, coughing. The guard on duty made his rounds; you could hear the clinking of his keys. Somebody in one of the farthermost cells shouted: 'Sick! Sick!'

Such is life. While some are in prison, others are laughing, exulting; some cry; many suffer. The prison exists because there are judges. It proves their diligence, their usefulness. One should visit hospitals, cemeteries, and prisons as one visits the historical monuments of a city. They are eloquent places – though in another way – and show the stage of maturity, of evolution, in a people. But everybody always wants to hide his blemishes, his deficiencies.

While a prisoner, Climbié, of all people, was a member of the Tribunal's flock. Each examining judge had his 'toadies' in the flock, and for each toady, the judge was a god one prayed to. But this god heard nothing. He hardly suspected the immense power ascribed to him, and which he had in actual fact. Guardian of the established order, he rarely understood how many miseries, dramas, and wasted lives there are in three years, ten years, fifteen years of prison! The Law is a numerical table. And one gets the impression now and then that man is made for the Law, that there is some sort of blank form which has to be filled out.

Freedom of opinion! Come on now! The right opinion is the opinion on the menu. Don't we see proof of it every day? Aren't we criticized even for our friendships?

[146]

All this talk about forming men of character. But now, who likes them? And Climbié looked at the faces of all these prisoners, invariably smiling. You would have thought they liked being in prison. And it was this casual smile which threw off the jailers. . . .

Climbié was finally free. One evening. With 'Exit Permit' in hand, he left. The street seemed too big for him. He turned around, stopped, and looked at the prison. And he said to himself: 'Men are still in there, men who, going to bed with the sun, want the night to go faster, and the day to be rather slow.' The air, blustering in gales, made it hard to breathe. He held it in his lungs, as if to wash away the miasma, the musty smells of the prison. He walked through the city like a stranger. He was free. And yet, he felt weighed down by all he had heard, by all that had been thrust upon his shoulders, the burden of a prison record. . . .

'Hey, you. . . . Stop!' shouted a policeman.

'What now?' muttered Climbié to himself, walking on since his exit permit was in hand.

'Hey, don't you listen when someone calls you? Don't you recognize me?'

The policeman he had passed by walked over to him. . . .

'Don't you recognize me? It's me, Dassi. . . .'

'Forgive me, my friend. I didn't recognize you. That uniform!'

'At last, it's over. . . .'

'Well yes . . . let's hope so. . . .'

'I became a policeman, you see.'

'A policeman who paints can't be very dangerous. Do you still paint?'

'I don't have time any more, alas. . . . Sometimes I feel like walking out, but I'm not single now.'

While talking, they had arrived in front of a bar, which they entered.

'So you don't dream any more, my friend. You refuse to live because you don't create any more; you don't want to commune with nature any more; don't you want to interpret things? Are you giving up?'

G

'No, I still have my brushes. And occasionally I feel something stirring inside me.'

'You're not altogether lost then.'

'And you? What happened to your books?'

'I sold them!'

'Sold them?'

'Yes, yes. It's a long story, but it's worth telling:

'Ah, no. it's not nice to return home empty-handed. It's even more painful to see old parents around you and young brothers holding out their hands, and have nothing to put in them. You want to give them something, so the smile blossoming on their lips will last a long time. And you dig into your pockets to no purpose, and the smiles, my dear friend, the smiles which had put joy in your heart, grow tired and fixed, then wilt, fall away, and die. I have seen those smiles, as radiant as the sun, die; and I said to myself every time, a rich man must be happy that, with a simple gesture, for him a trivial gesture, he is able, like a god, to make eyes sparkle and radiant smiles burst forth.

'When I came back to this country, I understood from the very first day that only wealth was valued.

'Then what good are old books and references in a city where only bank notes talk? Can you fight bank notes with books? And yet, books are a treasure, mines of inexhaustible wealth. Money being, from then on, the only argument that had any weight, I looked at these treasures of mine, which, in no circumstances, ever, would enable me – me too – to beat my chest like the others, with haughty self-assurance. I decided to sell them.

'Morning and evening, in front of my tray on the pavement, men passed by, swept up in the riotous rhythm of their lives. The books opened of themselves, as if to bridle everybody's indifference to them, as a frank, eloquent plea, a plea of despair, like a heart opening all of a sudden because it has waited so long, and doubted so long. One by one, the old books were opened; then people would pass on, seeming to say: "I see you've given up! What sort of wealth is that to display in public?"

'The books shrivelled up in the sun. The wind leafed through them, as if searching for a reference. I contented myself with reading and waiting. After I read, I would say to myself: "No, this one can still help me." And I would put it aside. At the end of the day, it turned out that all the books had been put aside. Yes, every one of them, all those shiny backs, like eyes that sparkle with intelligence, all those edges rough as rags, those bands jutting out like veins swollen with blood for ever young, those innumerable arabesques of decoration! All their ideas within reach of my hand! All those men, born on different continents, at different times, all those ideas begotten in habitats more or less rich, there, within my reach! I plundered them, greedy to become richer. But now, one day, which for me ought to be marked with a white cross, three young fellows examined several volumes and then went on their way, with black-market satchels under their arms. After that, a youngster came up and asked for "*Mamadou et Bineta*, the reader they use in primary schools in the black countries". I had in front of me, all mixed up, reverend patriarchs: Cicero, Racine, Chamfort, Goethe, Hugo, Chateaubriand, Schiller, Gautier, Maupassant, Flaubert. He also went on his way. Two Moslems left, unable to find the *Koran*. The shadows lengthened. No! night would not come without these books working their usual magic! What am I saying? But I knew it would happen! A teacher bought four books from me. In my naïveté I believed that he had just opened a flood-gate of curiosity, overturned the seats of indifference, shaken the foundation of mocking fortune, made a breakthrough to books, exorcized the evil spell. Alas! The men passed by now without even looking at me.

'The wind frisked about through the works, searching, it seemed, for a secret, a promise of peace, a word of hope which it then would take to the world, a word of gladness to place on the flowers where bees, butterflies, and poets would gather it, a sweet word to put on the lips of a child who would say it to his parents, a word of comfort to murmur in the ears of those who suffer, a word of life which would awaken laughter and bring back the savour of existence.'

'You only sold four books then?'

'But I am convinced that, in time, the bookshops and libraries will be more frequented, for the time is coming when genuine diplomas will be required of everybody.'

'Diplomas! my friend! How many men of real ability suffocate because they don't have an official pass to go exploring, through a thick foliage of parchments! Really now, what do you think about all the events you have lived through?'

'I have just come to realize that everything the European does in this country is a reflex action of self-defence: self-defence against the climate first, then against the men, the workers, the intellectual, the child who leaves for school, and even more, against the drums. To be sure, it will be some years before the child becomes a serious competitor – if they give him a chance to be one. But the drums!

'Studying our hearts, our spirits, our souls, in order to assimilate us completely, the European says to himself: "How can I dominate this country, these people, when every night the drums hold them to their ancestral language, bind them again to the past?"

'Round drums, drums in pairs, drums of all shapes and all tones, which night after night sound a call to assembly, transmitting messages faster than telegraph, swarming the news through villages of the dead, through villages of the living! True enough, not all the young people understand your language. But instinctively they answer: "Present!" You are part of our community. And your notes make more than one chord vibrate within them!

'Funeral drums and festival drums! You played in vain on 14 July and on 11 November, you beat out melodies dotted with French words, but in vain; you will remain essentially African and hold back our people at the edge of the bottomless abyss of depersonalization.

'Now, you sing only the joy of living together in peace. For you are no longer drums of war, but drums of joy, drums of life. . . .'

And taking out of his pocket a letter from M. Targe, Climbié began reading it to Dassi:

[150]

My dear Climbié,

I followed rather closely the events of these last years. In human relations it is always like this when men let themselves be guided solely by personal interests and desire for prestige.

In the interpenetration of races and peoples going on today, it is necessary, and we want it so, to give a leading role to knowledge, understanding, and love. . . .

You told me one day that one of your kings, when he took the throne, broke the tradition of waging war, despite the protests of certain chiefs. Well! this king acted wisely, since shortly thereafter, delegations from nearby kingdoms agreed to conclude a pact of alliance and non-aggression, even as they drank the old fetichistic toast.

And it was following his action that paths were beaten through all these regions, caravan paths, the paths of explorers.

Following the example of this king and our explorers, I say that we must go forward, boldly map out the paths which the new caravans will follow, the caravans of fraternity in a world at peace.

Abidjan, 18 April, 1953

NOTES

1. *Eburnéen*, sc., *eburné*, 'ivory-coloured'; used locally for the French *Ivoirien*, an inhabitant of the Ivory Coast.

2. See Appendix for a list of tribes (and languages) mentioned in *Climbié*, and their primary locations.

3. A waist-cloth which can be draped as a skirt or wrapped to form culottes.

4. Claude Favre, seigneur de Vaugelas (1585–1650), one of the founders of the *Académie Française*. In his *Remarques sur la langue française* (1647), he advocated a normative French grammar and language based upon the spoken usage at Court.

5. See n. 15 below.

6. See n. 9 below.

7. Long, loose-flowing smocks.

8. A water genie, well-known in the folklore of the peoples of the Ivory Coast and Ghana.

9. Talismans (Dadié's note). Probably refers to the Africans' pronunciation of 'charm'.

10. *Gnon*, in the Dioula dialect, means *fonio* (Dadié's note). In Fr. slang, 'biff, punch'. *Fonio* is a very common name in West Africa for a millet producing very fine grain used in couscous or in soups.

11. A sweet, berry-like fruit.

12. Date trees in the Ivory Coast are barely two metres high (Dadié's note).

13. Khorogo, now one of the principal cities of the Ivory Coast, located in the north-central region. It was founded about 1750 by the Kiembara tribe, and means 'Heritage' in their dialect (Tanga).

14. What grieves me is the thought of death,
   What grieves me is the thought of death, mami Amah,
   And that someone will throw sand over me (Dadié's note).
The song is in the N'zima dialect. Mami Amah, 'Mother Amah', is a popular generic name for woman.

15. During the colonial period, a French West African territory, whose chief officer was a Governor, was divided into *cercles* (areas or cities). At the head of each *cercle* was a white administrator, who came from the *Ecole Coloniale* in Paris. He took the semi-military title *Administrateur Commandant de Cercle*. The *cercles* were divided into *subdivisions*, each headed by a white *Chef*. The *Chefs de Subdivision* would, in general, pass exams to become *Administrateurs*. The *subdivisions* were divided into *cantons*, each headed by a Negro *Chef*. The *Chefs de Canton* had at their head a *Chef Supérieur*, also a Negro, who reported directly to the *Administrateur Commandant*. Thus were created two heirarchies, one Negro, one white. When there was a problem, the white *Commandant de Cercle* went to the white *Chef de Subdivision*, who went to the Negro *Chefs de Canton* who, in turn, went to the Negro *Chef Supérieur*, who then went back to the *Administrateur Commandant*.

16. C.F.A.O.– *Compagnie Française de l'Afrique Occidentale*
   S.C.O.A.– *Société Commerciale de l'Afrique de l'Ouest*
   C.I.C.A. – *Compagnie Industrielle et Commerciale de l'Afrique*
   C.F.C.I. – *Compagnie Française de la Cote d'Ivoire*
   C.R.O.A.– *Comptoirs Réunis de l'Ouest Africain*

17. A businessman who founded and maintained the Ivory Coast (Dadié's note). Arthur Verdier, a French naval officer, established in the 1860s a private trading company (*Compagnie de Kong*) which for several decades preserved the French presence in the face of the growing English threat, both military and commercial. In 1878, by his intrigues, he gained the title *Résident de France*; four years later he retired to France in great wealth, delegating the Company to his agents; his privileges were officially taken away in 1889. Meanwhile, however, and for whatever motives, he and his successors had founded the first coffee and cocoa plantations, explored the hinterlands, and, in general, prepared the way for the decree of 10 March, 1893, declaring the Ivory Coast a colony of France.

18. A student of the *Groupe Scolaire Central* (Dadié's note).

19. Another name for the N'zima tribe.

[154]

20. See n. 34 below.

21. A high plateau region in Guinea.

22. A region in Senegal, south of Gorée and Rufisque.

23. An Arabic expression from the Koran, meaning 'In the name of God'. It is usually followed by *Al rahman al rahim*, which means, 'God be praised and God be merciful'.

24. The best-known regiment of West African soldiers, founded originally by Faidherbe in Senegal. Tiaroye was in important *tirailleurs* garrison.

25. Among the Agni and N'zima tribes, when a man has died, the funeral ceremonies are held more than once. They are held in all the villages where the dead man has lived. And after the funeral ceremonies have been 'imported or exported' from village to village, and everybody has contributed to the expenses, there are always left-over funds to be divided up (Dadié's note).

26. Now called *Indemnité de Résidence*. During the colonial period, French West Africa was divided into economic 'zones'. The word 'zone' was also used for a cash allowance awarded to a civil servant. The amount varied according to the cost of living within the zone where the civil servant lived. The most expensive zone, Zone I, comprised the large capital cities like Dakar and Abidjan. The amount also varied with social status. Black Africans, living in Dakar, wanted a subsidy equal or comparable to that received by the Whites or Assimilated Blacks.

27. Member of a special caste, at once poet, musician, and sorcerer.

28. Louis-Léon-César Faidherbe (1818–89), French general, colonizer and Governor of Senegal (1854–61, 1863–65), and author of numerous books on African anthropology and language. He also explored the lagoon and coastal region of the Ivory Coast and followed the course of the Comoé River.

29. *Union Sénégalaise d'Industries Maritimes* (Dadié's note).

30. A ridge of hills so named because they resemble female breasts.

31. 'Let me live my life a little.' The chant is in the N'zima dialect.

32. French aviator who first succeeded, 12 May, 1930, in flying across the South Atlantic, from Saint-Louis in Senegal to Natal, Brazil, thus initiating intercontinental mail service long desired by the French. Passenger service was not begun until 1936.

33. In this instance, Moslem teachers, who are considered divine seers, capable of predicting the future. *Karamoko* is also the name, however, of a primitive warlike Negro people west of Kenya.

34. The name of an indigenous Liberian Negro people noted for their skill as boatmen. The chief tribal groups include the Kra, Bassa, Gi, and Gibbi.

35. A young mariner sixteen to eighteen years of age, ranking between cabin-boy and sailor.

36. N'zima etiquette requires a child, out of respect, not to have the same pillow as his elders (Dadié's note).

APPENDIX

A list of the tribes (and languages) mentioned in *Climbié*, and their primary locations.

Name of Tribe	Location
Fanti	The lagoon and coastal zone of the Ivory Coast.
Agni	The region between the Volta River (Ghana) and the Bandama River (Ivory Coast).
Baoulé	The savannah region of the Ivory Coast, between the N'zi and Bandama rivers.
N'zima	The lagoon and coastal zone of the Ivory Coast. Both Climbié and his creator, M. Dadié, are N'zima.
Bambara	Mali (formarly Sudan).
Dioula	Mali and the Ivory Coast; they are wandering merchants.
Hausa	Northern Nigeria and Niger.
Wolof	Senegal.
Anago	Nigeria.
Mossi	Upper Volta.
Cabrese	The northern part of Togo.
Peul	A large tribe, primarily cattlemen, found throughout French West Africa, but especially in Senegal, Mali, Upper Volta, Niger, and Dahomey.
Ewé	Ghana and Togo.
Ebrié	The lagoon and coastal zone of the Ivory Coast.